I0461617

TALES OF FAIRIES

The Tale of Rebecca THE Chased

This novel is a work of fiction. Names, characters, places and incidents either are the product of the author's imagination or are used fictitiously. Any resemblance to actual persons, living or dead, events or locales is entirely coincidental. Any person claiming otherwise is just plain silly.

© 2011 by Paul Rodriguez

All rights reserved. No part of this book may be reproduced or transmitted by any means, electronic or mechanical, including photocopying, recording, or by any information storage and retrieval system, without the express written consent of the Publisher, except where permitted by law. For information address: Renaissance Peak, Arvada Colorado.

ISBN: 0-9843281-4-9, 978-0-98432814-7

Printed in the United States of America

Cover Design by Deborah Miller

TALES OF FAIRIES

The Tale of
Rebecca
THE Chased

By Paul Vincent Rodriguez

 Renaissance Peak

In your eyes is a Gleem
And an energy Beam
That's as real as a Dream
We are all as we Seem
When we connect with our Eem

Special Thanks to:
Jamie Adler
Katherine Dockerty
Kathie Hall
Kailee Kemp
Lauren Martin
Blaire Rodriguez
Eileen Barker whose portrayal of a
Sexy Fairy inspired this character.
And, as always,
the fairies who trusted me with their stories.

The Tale of
The Tales of Fairies

It was late summer 2006 when I happened on a very rare occurrence. It was a fairy demotion. I watched as Qwendaline dropped her wings, bowed her head and grew from eighteen inches tall to almost six feet. She was now a human. Needless to say I was not supposed to see this but there I was among one hundred or so fairies of all types who now had to figure out what to do with me. After overcoming the shock and fear of a human wandering in on their ceremony, they accepted me as a friend.

Fairies are a very spiritual group. They believe that everything happens for a reason and that I must have a special purpose to have shown up during such a rare event. When they discovered I was a writer, they began telling me their stories.

Some told their stories reluctantly while others never seemed to stop talking. Every story was unique and carried a great message. Some of these stories helped me through difficult times in my own life. The story telling went on for months. About a year and a half after I met the fairies, I arrived at the clearing to find the entire group waiting for me. It was not another demotion. I stood nervously as the entire group fluttered up to my eye level and Qwendaline's mother, Grace, approached.

"You must go do your job now," she said softly.

"Am I no longer welcome here?" I asked.

"You are always welcome. But you have a job to do. The stories we have shared were not only for you. It is time to share them with others."

These are the Tales of Fairies as told to me by my friends in the clearing. Some stories are action packed while others are more cerebral. Some are about boys and some are about girls. I have tried to keep them short—like I said, some fairies tend to ramble—while maintaining the messages each thought important enough to share. I hope you enjoy reading the stories as much as I enjoyed hearing them.

Rebecca's Defining Moment

It was an unseasonably cold April morning in northern Georgia. But the week before had been warm and the week before that had seen seasonal rain so the flowers and trees were as colorful as expected around the local golf course on which humans were playing that game with a small white ball and a stick.

Tucked back into the hillside behind the flowers and trees that surround the thirteenth green was hidden a small birthing pond. In the trees surrounding the pond, in a private room with a view of the golf course, Michelle Duvall read the fine print on a contract she had just signed. She rolled the document up and wrapped a ribbon around it careful to balance the two loops of the bow she tied to secure it. She then tucked the small scroll into a burlap sack that hung from a nearby branch.

She adjusted herself on the bed of eucalyptus leaves rubbed with aloe vera gel and straightened her blanket. A Nurture Fairy fluttered in with a baby neatly bundled in a woven wool blanket.

"One moment," Michelle said as she reclined in the bed and propped her knees up in front of her. She reached out her hands and the caregiver gently laid the newborn in her arms.

"She is beautiful. What a face she has," said the Nurture Fairy.

"That's good," replied Michelle.

"I will return in a few minutes to help you with feeding."

"Thank you," said Michelle as the other fairy left the two alone. Michelle peeled back the blanket from the newborn's face. She smiled as she gingerly placed her daughter between her two raised legs which parted slightly creating a make-shift bassinet.

"Let's get a good look at you," Michelle said as she unwrapped the rest of the naked newborn and inventoried the baby's features.

"Let's start at your feet shall we? Ten toes is good. Not too long and not too chubby. Nice long legs. Let's hope we keep that going. Hips are nice and narrow."

Michelle lowered her left leg slightly causing the baby to roll in its bassinet displaying her profile. She ran her hand over the baby's bottom.

"Cute little butt. Could be an athlete but we won't let that get in the way."

Michelle reset her legs. The baby again faced forward.

"Small waist. Broad shoulders," Michelle smiled as small tears formed in the corner of her eyes, "And that face."

The baby fussed as Michelle gently closed the blanket leaving only the perfect face visible. She and the baby looked at each other.

"Looks like it's just you and me, but we will be okay. Your father has made sure you will have a good start. Given proper management and investing it will be just that—a good start. I will teach you everything I know. You, my dear, will do better than me. I promise, you will do better than me."

There was a gurgling sound followed by a small stream of baby urine that leaked out of the newborn's blanket and onto Michelle's nightgown. Michelle glanced at the mess and sighed, "I'm sorry you feel that way."

CHAPTER ONE

A Lady in Waiting

Mother raised me to be a proper lady: well-groomed, articulate, and polite. She also provided training in the art of seduction and flirtation. Training isn't really the correct term; it was more observation and mimicking on my part. It doesn't really matter how I came to have this knowledge, the important thing was that I had it. And while I would prefer to say that I earned each of my professional positions solely on my merits, I will admit that these special skills have served their purpose on an occasion or two or maybe more.

My education came in handy when I had my review with that ape they call a tooth fairy manager. I gave him the old "fake fatigue" routine: fake yawn, stretch my arms above my head then slowly out and gradually down to my side making sure to arch my back pushing my chest out (very important) and give him the "Oh, I'm sorry, I didn't get much sleep last night," with an impish grin. It's worked on every man but one and he didn't like girls. Little tools like that made me one of the most talked about fairies in the colony until Qwendaline got demoted and I'm not about to go through that just to be more popular. Besides, I was still the fastest tooth fairy in our colony though Brent might argue otherwise.

Popularity was never a big concern of mine anyway. I spent most of my life laying low and avoiding conflict afraid that someone might find out my secret; that my father had left my mom and me because his parents didn't think Mother was good enough for him. I guess I'm fortunate that she didn't choose to take the special herbs that could have prevented me altogether. But I guess, like Aynil says, "everything happens for a reason."

You can't pick your family. More philosophical beings working on a different spiritual plane may say otherwise like, "your soul chooses to come to this earth and puts itself into the body of the being whose life will provide the situations needed for your spirit to learn what it seeks." I don't think I'm quite ready to believe all of that. I don't think I would choose to be born to a single mother whose primary goal it was to teach me how to catch a rich man. Of course I doubt it was Mother's first choice to raise a daughter as a single parent. I'm sure both of us being placed into a situation that neither preferred was the key to how our life together would evolve.

When there are only two of you, each trial, each test is more focused and direct. You can't complain to a sibling about your parents. You can't direct a problem to another parent that you think will be more understanding. It was Mother and me against the world. As long as we had each other, we would be fine. But it was the "me against Mother" conflicts during my school years that affected us the most. It all seemed to start when I was four.

CHAPTER TWO

The Chaser and the Chased

"It's not safe," I thought. It was never safe as long as he was still around. I was smart enough not to sit on a perch but the safe spot was a long way away and numerous branches lay in between. It was dusk and I knew Mother would be calling me soon. He knew it too. Like a cat, he was lurking out there somewhere. It wouldn't be long before he made his move. I worried that my hair might get in my face or I might snag my new dress on a branch. You see, I wasn't supposed to be there.

Mother thought I was at Remi's house playing with dolls or having a tea party or something silly that girls do. And I *was* there for a while but it got boring. Remi had a weird sense of humor and always made me play her mother and her brother always wanted to be the kitty. I never understood the kitty part. Anyway, mother put me in my newest dress—even though I told her I might spill tea on it—and wouldn't let me wear a pony tail or pull my hair back. So here I was, in the last game of Touch-and-Go of the night, dressed for a tea party.

I heard the buzz of his frantically flapping wings coming from above and a moment later Brent smacked me on the top of my head and yelled, "What'cha doin?" The race was on. Like swallows we jetted toward the safe spot swooping and slaloming through the tree branches before us. I knew this path. I used it often.

First I had to maneuver through three fir trees which had fairly well-spaced limbs that were, at best, four inches thick. I would speed up heading into the medium-sized Cottonwood which wasn't really considered an obstacle because of the wide spacing of its branches. Next I swooped down and under the grove of seven Aspen trees of assorted sizes. While Aspens are a great place to hide, the dense foliage and close proximity of the trees makes them nearly impossible to fly through. I would have to shoot upward immediately after clearing the Aspens in order to avoid the low canopy of the Apple trees and align myself with the safe spot.

The safe spot was an area measuring two leaves by four leaves with the letters S-A-F-E carved into the trunk of the giant Cottonwood. The small target is about two-thirds of the way up the tree that stands at the center of the colony. I would be fine as long as no new branches had grown in the previous two days. I should have been winning easily but I couldn't tell. Brent was nowhere to be seen.

Brent was the only other four-year-old in the colony allowed to be out this late. He and I played together all the time when we first got our wings. We seemed to get the hang of flying quicker than the other kids. So while the others were still flying tethered to their parents, Brent and I were checking out the lower elevations in the forest. We got really good at flying straight up when our parents called so they wouldn't think we had dropped below the lower branch line. The lower branch line was where cats usually could be found. Brent was the second best flyer of our age. I, of course, was the best but I had to beat him to the safe spot or I would have to relinquish that title until we played Touch-and-Go again. Where was he? Once again, he came from above.

Brent dove from the top of the Aspens and met me half way across the top of the Apple trees. We were now neck and neck. The buzzing of our wings grew as the flapping became more violent. Getting hair in my face was no longer a concern. At this speed, it just trailed behind me like a jet stream. He was NOT going to beat me. There was no way I was going to be caught; especially not by one boy and in the last game of the day.

I thrust my right hand out and tried to knock him off course but he slid away at the last moment and the shove turned into more of a useless tap. We neared the end of the Apple trees in record time. Only a small clearing ahead before we reached the giant Cottonwood. Brent was still beside me. Any small mistake would mean defeat. This was going to be close. I closed my eyes and squeezed my whole body to pull any extra energy I could out of my wings.

RIP! I heard. He must have caught his shirt or pants on a branch. "I've got him now," I thought. Our hands stretched out before us - my right hand and his left as we positioned ourselves on either side of the large tree trunk. Both slapped the word "safe" at the same time and our momentum carried us into the surrounding branches of the Cottonwood as we slowed down. The argument of who won started immediately after the hands touched the tree.

"Ha!" I yelled. "You still can't catch me!"

"I won!" protested Brent. "My hand hit first!"

"No!"

"Yes!"

"Nuh uh!"

"Uh huh!"

"I heard it," I argued. "My hand slapped first, then yours."

7

"Then your ears aren't very good because my hand hit a tiny bit before yours," he returned.

"No!"

"Yes!"

"Nuh uh!"

"Uh huh!"

"There's no way you could beat me! I heard your clothes rip!" I proclaimed.

"My clothes didn't rip!" he replied. "Yours did!"

"Nuh uh!"

"Look!" he said and pointed to the two-inch-long tear in the trim at the bottom of my new dress and the corresponding scrape on my thigh. My dress had caught on a new stub of a branch that had just grown out of one of the larger tree limbs. It was my new dress. It was for school. And it was one of Mother's favorites. She was going to be very disappointed. She might even yell at me. I hated when she yelled at me—not so much because she was yelling but because I knew that she only yelled when she was the most disappointed. And while I often did things that she did not approve of, I did those things because I enjoyed them and not because they would disappoint her. She did not approve of me playing Touch-and-Go.

She thought it wasn't lady-like. But flying and chasing was in my blood. Maybe it came from my father who I didn't know. Maybe it was in a recessive gene on my mother's side. I didn't know where it came from. All I knew was that I was, and still am, a good athlete. I enjoyed flying fast and I had never been caught. But none of that mattered at the time. My dress was torn and Mother would be upset. I started to cry.

Brent didn't know what to do. I think he thought he hurt me. He looked scared and nervous.

"What happened?" he asked. "Are you hurt? I'll get my mom."

"I tore my dress," I whined. Brent was even more confused. We tore clothing all the time. That's what happens when you spend your life weaving through branches at high speeds. It's also why fairy clothes are always shredded on the sleeves and pant legs unless, of course, you are my mother who somehow avoided all the branches and leaves.

"It's just a dress," said Brent.

"This is my new dress for the first day of school tomorrow," I wept. "Mother is going to be mad!"

"Oh no! School is tomorrow," shouted Brent. "I have to go. Bye." That quickly, Brent was gone, leaving me to face Mother, alone.

CHAPTER THREE

The Power of the Eem

*T*meekly fluttered through the front door of our house to find Mother and Mr. Brock talking. The subject must not have been that important to Mother since the conversation stopped when she turned around and saw me not at all dressed the way she had sent me out earlier that day. Her eyes scanned me from head to knee—that is where she saw the scrape on my leg and the tear in my dress. I will always remember the look of disappointment on her face. That look was the thing I least wanted to see. The look meant so much more than disappointment. It meant I had done something wrong; and not just something wrong but something I knew better than to do. It meant I had made a poor decision or, to put it bluntly, I had been stupid. Worst of all, *I* knew I had made the poor decision. *I* knew I had been stupid and that knowledge made me upset with myself.

I didn't need to hear her speak, I could feel her eem. Our eems were strong with each other as they typically are between parents and young children. The eem is our power to connect emotionally and spiritually with another fairy. It allows us to see and feel first-hand another fairy's thoughts and emotions. The power of one's eem between one's self and another fairy is most affected by three things.

First, and most important, is the level of focus one has with the fairy with whom they are engaged. The strongest connections are made when both fairies are focused on each other. Distractive thoughts that pull your attention away from the other fairy weaken the eem and lessen the experience being shared. Very strong eem connections have been described as having the ability to read the other fairy's mind.

The second factor is truth or honesty and the sharer's commitment to the story. Lies tend to have weak eem commitments. The more we share our experiences with others, the more familiar they become with our eems and the harder it becomes to successfully lie to them. That is why fairies can usually tell when you are lying and why we tend to fall for the lies of strangers more than the lies of those closest to us. The only things that have been proven to inhibit our ability to spot inconsistent eems are love and infatuation. Love and infatuation tend to "cloud" the air around us fogging our judgment as well as our eeming ability.

The third factor takes into the account how many times the experience has already been shared. With stories, the more they are told, the less emotional the teller typically is. This is why simply talking about traumatic experiences helps us to get past them and ultimately move on. Unfortunately, the more joyous experiences also tend to fade although not as quickly. Traveler fairies are noted for their ability to maintain a strong eem over many years so as to help others better re-live the Traveler's past as he or she re-tells their stories over and over again. At that moment I wished I was a Traveler. I started crying again.

"Oh, Rebecca," she sighed as she fluttered toward me, "what happened to you?"

"I'm sorry," I cried.

"This didn't happen at Remi's, did it?" she said.

"No."

"Were you playing Touch-and-Go again?"

"Yes," I whimpered.

"Rebecca, this is your new dress," she reminded me with that familiar tone of disappointment that was usually followed by a sigh.

"I'm sorry," I whimpered again.

She brushed the loose leaves and dirt from my dress and turned my tearful face toward her. She could feel the remorse in my eem. She pulled me into her, wrapped her arms around me and held me. "I know," she said. Then, with two quick pats on the butt, she pushed me away from her and toward the bathroom and said, "Now, go get ready for your bath. I will be in after I finish with Mr. Brock." I watched as she changed from compassionate mother to flirtatious negotiator in an instant. All I cared about was that she wasn't mad at me.

I hung the dress on a hanger and laid out my pajamas as I listened to Mother's voice change from proper-speaking parent to a sultry Southern Belle.

"Brock, I do appreciate your offer," she fawned. "I just don't want people thinking I took advantage of your kindness."

"I'm not worried about what other people think," he smugly said.

"Well, thank you," she said. "I am anxious to see your work first-hand."

"You won't be disappointed," he said confidently.

"I'm certain I won't be," she said. "I hope you don't think me rude by asking you to leave but I have to tend to my daughter. Tomorrow is her first day of school."

"I understand," said Brock.

"What day did you say you would be starting, again?"

"Right away," he answered while being led toward the door. "I will come by tomorrow."

"Tomorrow? That soon?" she asked.

"It's best to get it done and cured before the weather sets in," he explained.

"Can you be here before high sun?" she inquired. "It would make my day a little easier if you can get started early."

"Of course," said Brock with a smile.

"You truly are a gentleman in every sense of the word," praised Mother as she briefly rubbed his shoulder and pushed him toward the open front door. "You have a safe flight home, now."

"I will," he said.

"Goodnight," Mother smiled.

"Goodnight," Brock smiled back.

That was the beginning of the five-year remodel that would become Mother's bedroom suite.

Mother and I laughed and played in the bath and she and I read a story before I fell asleep on her lap. I woke up to find my dress cleaned and pressed and missing the tear in the trim I had created the night before. As it turned out, Mother was very good with a needle and thread. My dress looked new which was important to Mother. Proper fairies did not wear torn clothes to school—especially not on the first day.

CHAPTER FOUR

Making Friends and Influencing People

"*N*o, her name is Rebecca," was Mother's reply to my new teacher's question of, "Can I call you Becky?" The question was asked in that overly sweet, high-pitched tone used so prevalently on young children. It was the question that was always asked whenever I met someone for the first time and Mother's answer was always the same. Mother thought that Beckys, Beccas, Rebas, or those with any other derivation of my name were simple people with no self-esteem, destined to be cheerleaders and waitresses. They were the kind of girls who were immature and flirtatious and would make themselves appear dumb to impress boys. They were common. So while as a kindergartener I kind of liked the name Becky, I was doomed to be a Rebecca.

My first day of school, after Mother left, was filled with excitement and learning and meeting new kids who cared only that I was polite and fun and not afraid to be there, unlike some of the other kids. Like the kids who cried every time their parents dropped them off, or the ones who couldn't bring themselves to play with the plethora of toys now at their disposal but instead just stood silently in a corner hoping no one would talk to them.

The first few weeks were spent adjusting to the many personalities in the room. The playground nets were kept low at recess—if flying was allowed at all— and there was absolutely no Touch-and-Go. Making friends was easy for anyone who tried. Brent did especially well considering he was one of the smaller boys in the class. Everyone thought he was cool because he never let anything bother him, had a good sense of humor, and wasn't afraid to stand up for himself. He didn't get in fights but would tell the others to stop doing things he didn't like. When you are young, people respect your wishes more than when you are a teenager. Brent also had a catch phrase—"what'cha doin'?"—that he used instead of offering a simple "Hello." It wasn't so much the words that were cool but that he could say it a hundred different ways. One time he would jump up behind you and blurt it out quickly and another time he might sneak up next to you at rest period and whisper it in your ear. All the boys thought it was cool and it made most of the girls giggle. I'd heard it all before.

It was the fourth week when Jarfer, ripped the Carlin the Traveler doll from my hands and I got angry and cried. My crying drew the immediate attention of Miss Loni, my teacher, who then displayed her great disappointment with Jarfer by grounding him to the corner for five minutes. Grounding, or denying someone the right to fly, is the worst punishment a fairy can receive. Kailee and Cora were the first of my classmates to check on me.

"What happened?" asked Kailee.

"Jarfer took Carlin from me," I sobbed.

"Oh," they both said and then flew off to play in the kitchen area. I'm sure you can see how that could be the start of two great friendships. That day the three of us flew home together.

"Want to hear my new word?" asked Cora rhetorically. She turned and hovered in front of Kailee and me and blurted, "Scritching. It's when you scratch an itch. Get it? You can say you're scritching instead of scratching and itching."

"That is so cool!" shouted Kailee and she started scratching her leg. "Look at me, I'm scritching my leg."

"I'm scritching my arm," said Cora as she scratched her forearm.

"Now I'm scritching my belly," called Kailee.

"And now I really need some scritching on my feet," said Cora.

I watched as Kailee and Cora scratched themselves all over as we flew to their homes. Kailee and Cora were neighbors and had been all their lives. Kailee was two months older than Cora and reminded her of that fact whenever they got into a dispute over who should get first choice in things. Both Kailee and Cora were greeted at their doors by female parents who were shocked to see their daughter's bodies pink from head to toe.

"Hi Mommy," both Kailee and Cora said.

"What happened to you?" their mothers asked in unison as they began examining their children's scratched bodies. Cora tried to go into the house but her mother said, "You stay out here until we figure out what's wrong with you."

"We were scritching," said Kailee.

"It's my new word," gleamed Cora.

"What is scritching?" asked Cora's mother.

"It is when you are scratching an itch," replied Cora proudly.

"Does your body itch all over?" asked a worried Kailee's mother.

"It does now," said Kailee.

"What do you mean? Did it itch all day? When did it start itching?" inquired her mother.

"It started itching after we started scritching," said Kailee.

"So you didn't have an itch until you scratched yourself?" asked Cora's mom.

"Mommy, it's scritching," corrected Cora.

"So you didn't fly into any poison ivy or poison oak?" confirmed Kailee's mom.

"No and we didn't go near the creek either just like you always tell us," said Kailee.

"Good. I'm glad you remembered that. We'll have to put some aloe on these scratches," said Kailee's mom as she noticed me for the first time. "Who is that?" she asked Kailee.

"That's Rebecca," said Kailee.

"That's Rebecca," said Cora to her mom. "She's a new friend from school."

"How is it you didn't get all scratched up?" Cora's mom asked me.

"I didn't have anything that needed scritching," I replied.

"I'm glad to see you've picked a smart new friend," said Kailee's mom to her pink, itchy daughter. She turned to me, "Would you like to come in for a snack?"

"No thank you ma'am. Mother is expecting me at home," I replied politely.

"What's your mom's name?" she asked.

"My mother is Michelle Duvall," I answered.

"I don't think I know your mom. Maybe we could all get together some time?"

"Okay," I said.

"We'd better get these two inside and get some medicine on them," said Kailee's mom.

"I'd better get home, too," I said.

"Do you live far? Do you want someone to go with you?" asked Cora's mom.

"No, thank you. I don't live very far."

"Okay then. Be careful going home," said Kailee's mom.

"I will," I said then exchanged cheerful "good-byes" with my new friends and turned toward home.

CHAPTER FIVE

Homework

I arrived at the front door of my typically empty house as I heard the familiar buzzing of Brent's wings closing in from behind.

"Rebecca, what'cha doin'?" he hollered as he approached.

"Hi Brent," I said.

"Hey, you wanna play Touch-and-Go?"

"I can't."

"Why not?"

"Because Mother said I can't after school. I have homework."

"Homework?" said Brent, "We didn't get homework."

"It's not from school," I replied.

"Oh," he said. "Maybe you can play later?"

"Maybe."

"Okay. See you later."

"Bye."

Homework, again, just to be clear, was not homework from school. Just to be more clear, this was not housework like washing dishes or doing laundry. My homework was stuff Mother had designed to make me a "proper fairy." Things like articulation and annunciation, reading, vocabulary, and walking. Walking was the one thing I practiced mostly on my own. Fairies didn't typically walk unless they were stuck in a place too small to fly or they were at some rich fairy ball where they liked to show off the skills they developed with the spare time they had because they didn't have to work.

Only very rich fairies walked gracefully because most had been practicing walking since they were six-years-old. I was five.

First I ambled through the sparsely decorated living room that had a soft perch and my grandmother's rocking perch and reading table where Mother would read to me before bed. I staggered through the small kitchen with its triangle-shaped table and three perches and our old cooking element and cooling box. I stumbled and tripped up the stair frame to the new addition that would someday be Mother's bedroom and bathroom. This was what she and Mr. Brock were talking about the day before school when I tore my dress. Mother and he seemed to spend a lot of time together. Mr. Brock had recently started a building company and this was one of his first projects. The room was only structurally thatched right now because Mr. Brock left before it was done. I thought it was interesting that he would leave after only building the floor support system. Since Mother consistently claimed we had no extra money, I assumed Mr. Brock did the work for free. Mother had a way of getting men to do things for free.

I stumbled back down to the main floor and the bedroom we shared and collapsed on the small bed that was mine. Walking is hard work and I needed to rest. I stared into the small, perfectly organized, closet. My clothes hung on two rungs. Those that had not been caught or snagged while flying through trees, also known as "school clothes", hung from the top. There were five dresses, three pair of shorts and seven tops of assorted colors and patterns that could be arranged into a number of different outfits. The small row of "play clothes" that were represented by pants, tops and the occasional dress that had a rip or tear but nowhere near as damaged as those worn by my friends, hung closer to the floor. Beside my clothes hung Mother's navy blue dress with big white flowers and her classic burlap dress. She wore the burlap one the most. She said it didn't show wear as much. I laid there looking at her two home-made dresses. Neither had a tear or rip anywhere.

As I rested, I remembered the events of the day but my mind stuck on one word—mommy. Kailee and Cora call their mothers "mommy." What's a "mommy" or a "mom" for that matter? Kailee's mommy had asked who my "mom" was.

I was always instructed to call my mother, "Mother." It is proper and what proper people do. I think the term "proper people" was more a reference to rich people than people who do things correctly.

I wanted a mommy. I wanted someone who would play games with me and tickle me and tell stories with me and not care if my clothes got dirty. I wanted some- one who didn't care that I was the best dressed or the smartest or the most polite and articulate. And I really didn't want to have to walk anymore. My feet and legs hurt and who cared anyway. We weren't rich and I wasn't going to a ball any time soon. I just wanted Mother to let me be a kid like Kailee and Cora and Brent. I wanted her to let me do things on a whim and not have to plan my playtime or schedule play dates. I wanted her to let me speak with poor grammar and mumble and slur my words. I wanted her to expect less of me and hold me to a standard similar to the other kids in school who don't have to get good grades and who get to miss class to go watch the moth hatch on the river. And I want- ed her to let me call her "Mom" or "Mommy" or something softer and more adoring than "Mother." Where did the idea of calling her Mother come from anyway? No one I knew did it and I haven't heard it used in any of the tales I've heard the Traveler tell. But after thinking about it, I think I would have been more willing to do all of those things—walk, speak properly, be the smartest kid in the class and even call her Mother—if she would just let me play Touch-and-Go.

My thoughts were interrupted by the sound of Mother coming in the front door. Through the bedroom door I watched her float toward the kitchen with a bag of groceries. Perfectly quaffed as usual, she wore her white, sleeveless dress with the bold flower pattern. Her shoulder length hair was pushed back with a headband. The small amounts of sunlight that came through the windows glistened off her hair like a halo so that, even while carrying groceries, she looked like an angel.

"Rebecca?" she called.

"I'm in bed," I replied.

She floated to the door. Her face was more inquisitive than caring as she asked, "Are you okay? Are you sick?"

"I'm just tired. I was walking," I answered.

"Good," she said, then spun effortlessly in the air. "Come help me with dinner."

I dragged myself from the bed and fluttered toward the kitchen where I snapped the stems off asparagus.

"How was your day?" Mother asked.

"Good," I replied.

"Did you learn anything new?"

"No, just the same letters and numbers."

"Did anyone fall down?" she asked with a grin.

"No. But Jarfer was grounded for five minutes," I replied to the unusual question.

"Five minutes," Mother said surprised. "That's a pretty long time. What did he do?"

"He took the Carlin doll away from me."

"He took the Carlin doll away?"

"I was playing with the Carlin the Traveler doll and he just came up and took it," I explained.

"What did you do?" Mother asked.

"I cried," I mumbled,

"What was that?" she again inquired.

"I cried," I articulated.

Mother rolled her eyes with disapproval. Even though she could feel my sadness through my eem, she was always disappointed when I let other people upset me.

"But it worked," I defended. "Miss Loni came over and got Carlin back for me and grounded Jarfer for five minutes."

"Did that make you happy?"

"What?"

"Did it make you happy to have someone fix your problem for you?"

"Yes," I said, embarrassed. I don't know why I was embarrassed. I mean, come on, I was five-years-old. It seemed like a lot to ask for me to resolve every conflict

26

I was going to encounter at that age. I understood the concept of standing up for myself but boys are generally more aggressive than girls and the stuff I watched Mother do to manipulate men wasn't going to work for another eight years; six years at best.

For the next minute or so all that was heard in the kitchen was the sound of asparagus stems being snapped off and the sound of water spilling into a pot. "Jarfer has always been a bit of a nuisance anyway," Mother said almost smiling. "I'm not surprised, with the parents he has. Go get your books ready. We'll do your other lessons after dinner."

"Then can I go play?"

"Go play? Where?"

"Brent wants to play Touch-and-Go," I said excitedly.

"I doubt you will have time for that. It is a school night and you need to have a bath."

"Then can I play at someone else's house?"

"And who would that be?" she asked with a noted interest.

"I made two friends today at school—Kailee and Cora."

"It's about time you got some girl friends," Mother said with relief.

"We flew home together," I interjected. "They live close."

"Are they expecting you?"

"No."

"Then let's do it another day when we can plan something," she said.

"When can we plan something?" I asked.

"Maybe this weekend," offered Mother.

That night I learned to articulate the word anticipation—the definition of which was now best represented by the phrase "maybe this weekend." Mother gave me a long bath; careful to lather, rinse and condition my perfectly groomed hair. When I was dry and properly pajama'ed, Mother got out the hair brushes and did one hundred strokes with each as I stared out the window at the other kids playing Touch-and-Go until the sun finally set over the mountains. I miss playing Touch-and-Go. I miss having someone brush my hair, too.

CHAPTER SIX

Touch-and-Go

ouch-and-Go is a flying game that humans might equate to a combination of Tag and Hide-and-Seek. Touch-and-Go can be played individually or in teams. The game starts by everyone gathering at the safe spot. Everyone spreads out in the field staying inside the exterior boundaries set up at the start of the game. If you go outside the boundaries you are considered caught or a cheater—neither of which is good. Each player tries to tag another player and fly to the safe spot before the player they tagged gets there. If the tagged person doesn't beat the tagger to the safe spot, they are caught and must go to the Caught branch and wait until a teammate catches someone from the other team. If you are playing singles, you have to wait for the next game. If the tagged person reaches the safe spot first, the game continues as before. Sometimes, to speed up the game, we play whoever loses the race to the safe spot is caught. The game is over when everyone from one team is caught. It was the most popular thing to do during school recess and a game for fast and agile flyers, like me.

It was second grade and the school playground net was set high giving the players an even larger boundary area. Again Mother had dressed me in her favorite dress; this one was baby blue with ruffled sleeves. I still remembered the day before kindergarten and the accident I had with Brent. I wasn't taking that chance again. So I was stuck having another fake tea party with some lame girl while Kailee and Cora got to chase the boys under the extra high net. They were playing boys against the girls and the girls weren't having any luck. They needed me. I was still the fastest fairy in our age group. I could catch anyone—even Brent who would occasionally fly by and holler "what'cha doin'" to taunt me.

Kailee and Cora, who weren't great athletes to begin with, were getting too tired to catch their opponents. The boys began calling them owls and albatrosses and names of other less agile birds. One flew up to Cora, held out his finger to within an inch of her nose and said, "I'm not touching you." I couldn't sit there any more. I had to do something to get into the game but Mother would kill me if I ripped this dress. The answer was in my hand.

If I spilled something on me, Miss Helen would give me the spare clothes they keep for kids who have accidents. They were already shredded. The tea was just dark enough to make a mess but not so much as to do permanent damage. I asked for a refill from my gracious but lame hostess, put the cup to my lips, and faked a huge cough. The tea splashed down the front of my dress. I jumped up showing what I thought to be the correct amount of surprise and anguish. Within minutes I was changed into the spare clothes and darting toward the branches. I rose up into the middle of the playing area and placed my hand on the safe spot.

"Watch out you guys, she's really fast," warned Brent.

All of the boys laughed then watched as I darted to the boy farthest away, touched him on the nose and shot back to the safe spot before the touched boy could blink. Their jaws dropped. They were all in shock and I got two more out before their mouths closed. The recess bell sounded with all the girls free and only Brent to capture. The after-recess snack was especially sweet that day.

Back home, I made sure my dress had not been damaged too badly. Most of the tea had already come out with a simple rinsing. I would be okay. I did my homework right away and again collapsed on my bed exhausted from my walking exercises. I even tried dancing a little that time because walking was getting a lot easier.

"Rebecca?" Mother called sternly. She had seen the dress.

"I'm on my bed," I called back.

"What happened to your dress?" she inquired.

Now that I think about it, she never said things like "what did you do to this?" or "why did you do that?" I think she either wanted to give me the benefit of the doubt or she didn't think I ever did anything wrong. I'm guessing it was the former. Or maybe she didn't care whose fault it was and just wanted the details so she could get on with solving the problem. But I digress.

"What happened to your dress?" she inquired. She turned the corner of the room and was startled by the borrowed clothes I was wearing. "Oh, goodness," she said. "Where did those rags come from?"

"They're the spare clothes from the school," I answered somewhat proudly.

"Remind me to send some spare clothes with you this week."

"Can they be torn ones that I can wear at recess?" I pleaded. "I want to play Touch-and-Go with the other kids."

"Is that how this happened?" she asked as she held up the dress.

"We were having a tea party," I replied.

"I will never understand why they let you use real tea for those things," she said shaking her head. "It looks like it will come out easily enough. I can wash it in the creek tomorrow. Change out of those clothes so I can wash them before we send them back and come help me with dinner."

"Can I take some play clothes to school?" I asked again. I hated wearing good clothes to school. I wasn't very thrilled with school altogether. Class wasn't a challenge and most of the kids were immature so the only thing to look forward to was recess and flying with my friends. Sometimes it physically hurt to sit and watch the games from the ground knowing that I would have an impact on the outcome. I needed to play. I needed her to say yes.

"You can take something that isn't too ripped up," she answered reluctantly. "We'll see if we can find something that is just starting to fray a little."

I was so happy I almost flew through the roof. "Thank you, thank you, thank you," I repeated as I gave her a giant hug.

"Those clothes will come straight home if even one grade drops," she reminded.

"Okay," I said.

"I mean it," she said sternly.

"I understand," I said. "I promise it won't hurt my grades." And it didn't.

33

I showed up to school the next day with two sets of play clothes and a new attitude. And while school still had a tough time challenging me or keeping my attention, the threat of losing recess privileges scared me enough to pay attention and do my homework. Brent was the only boy happy to see me on the field. Boys still have a hard time getting beat by girls in any sport but Brent and I were still pretty evenly matched so I didn't intimidate him. One time he and I took on the rest of the class. We won easily but we were all just kids and didn't yet know about strategy or plays that could isolate faster players. We wouldn't stand a chance even two years later.

That year I wore out two sets of play clothes and came home with a couple pretty good scratches Mother didn't appreciate. In third grade I would scrape both of my knees as I went through a growth spurt and now had longer and less coordinated appendages to drag behind me. The long legs also made walking hard again. I spent extra time after school the next two years attempting to become even more graceful which, as it turned out, is great for your leg muscles. By the end of fourth grade, I had sufficiently strengthened my legs and my wings, which now had to carry the extra weight. By the start of fifth grade, Touch-and-Go was becoming less and less important to those who did not excel at it and other things began to take its place. Life was going to be very different from here on out.

CHAPTER SEVEN

Boys? Seriously?

I was in fifth grade when I came home from school to find Mother talking with Will who would complete the final phase of construction of the bedroom addition. I measured my elementary school years by the men Mother hung out with and the progress of the bedroom suite. Kindergarten was Brock who did the framing. Framing entailed thatching sticks to living branches of a tree that have been treated to avoid future growth in certain places so as to not disrupt the next phases of construction. This process allowed for flooring to be installed which was done by Thurm during first grade. Flooring is thatching sticks and twigs to the structural floor frame. The sticks are then sanded and waxed to prevent rot and unintentional foot poking.

Second grade was Darcy and the walls and roof. The walls and roof were made by weaving reeds, tall grasses and stalks into a mesh of branches and sticks attached to the floor and waxed on the outside for water resistance. Incorporated into the walls were two windows and one door which were installed by James during third grade. Windows and doors were the only things we used that were taken from human design and were considered status symbols in our world. The wealthy could have as many as four windows and a solid wood door with hinges in their house while the less fortunate in our community might have only one doorway that was covered by a blanket in the winter.

Fourth grade was Bob and interior finish. He would prepare a plaster of mud, leaves and grass that he smoothed over the woven interior walls and ceiling that made the inside look like a human home. Fifth grade she had two things completed; Simon installed the rain water capture system that was as close to indoor plumbing as humans have and Will created the cloaking drape that every fairy home has. The drape needs to be renewed every twenty years or so or it will start to fail. Humans may catch a glimpse of a fairy house out of the corner of their eye when a cloaking drape is not working correctly. Usually the device is working properly by the time the human looks back. A good cloaking drape can last one hundred years. Will was making us his very best.

I learned to not get attached to these father figures but still tried to learn what I could from each of these experts while they were around. Mostly I watched how

Mother treated them. She was pleasant and considerate and accommodating. She made them feel strong and smart and necessary and she was able to do this without pretending to be stupid or giving them a single kiss on the lips. It was amazing to watch. Will completed the drape quickly and Mother moved her bed up to the new bedroom. For the first time, I had my own room.

Mother's male friends weren't the only markers in the timeline of my life. I also measured my years by my changing levels of interest in boys. Grades one and two, boys were just girls with different parts. Grade three they started to look cute. Grade four they were something to tease if you liked one. By fifth grade conversations with friends seemed to focus on the opposite sex more and more. At least that's how it was for Kailee. I still maintained my skepticism about the male gender in general but made a couple exceptions. I had great respect for the boys who could keep up with me on the Touch-and-Go field. Brent and I were still pretty good friends. Cora's interest in boys was somewhere between me and Kailee. She seemed very cautious when it came to making a commitment. It all came to a head in grade six on Saint Patrick's Day.

"Roses are red and violets are blue, I got all my money and your money too. Signed Seamus," recited Cora.

"I think it's your best ever," sang Kailee. "Okay,

check this out. 'All you humans think you are so smart but you're really dumber than the moss on the trees.' Signed Angus."

"Ouch!" I said.

"A little harsh, don't you think?" said Cora.

"They're humans who also believe in leprechauns, duh," Kailee exclaimed. "Serves them right."

"You could've at least made it rhyme," added Cora.

Saint Patrick's Day was my second favorite human holiday after Halloween. On Saint Patrick's Day we would trip the human's leprechaun traps, take the money, leave nasty notes and blame it on leprechauns— one of which I have still yet to see. On Halloween, we got to actually go out and fly around the humans and they just thought we were decorations.

"What you got, Rebecca?" asked Kailee.

I cleared my throat. I recited,

> "There is a little green man
> Who always takes all that he can
> He will take all your money
> And think it is funny
> Then run as fast as he can."

"A limerick. Very clever," said Cora.

"You used 'can' twice," said Kailee.

"I know. It was the best I could do on short notice,"

I said. "I had a bunch of homework tonight."

"Did you get all that math done?" asked Cora. "There were like twenty questions."

"And I had nature science," I said. "I had to get five different types of tree bark."

"Wait, wait, wait," interrupted Kailee, "we were supposed to get tree bark?"

"The assignment said to bring in five different barks. What kind of bark did you think?" I asked.
Kailee burst out laughing. Cora and I looked at each other for a reason for the sudden outburst. "Why are you laughing?" I asked Kailee.

Kailee giggled, "You wanna hear my impersonation of a Chihuahua?" Then she barked like a tiny dog.
Cora and I erupted with laughter. I laughed so hard that I almost fell off the branch I was perched on. Cora started to hyperventilate. The three of us bounced around yapping and barking like dogs for the next couple of minutes. We began to calm ourselves and were almost back to normal when Kailee said, "No, no, no. Check this one out. It's really good. It is a Rottweiler."

Kailee set herself, took a deep breath, and let go a deep, angry bark that sounded just like a Rottweiler. Cora and I sat in amazement for a moment until, all of a sudden, the real dogs from the surrounding houses starting barking and we all burst out laughing again.

We eventually gathered ourselves then flew off together into the chilly night air and amongst the trees with new leaves bursting from the previously bare branches. Below us bushes and early tulips bloomed and above us was the glow of a full moon. We didn't really intend on tripping many leprechaun traps, we just wanted the freedom of going out at night on our own. Everything was light and normal until Kailee asked Cora and me what we thought about going out with a boy. To make it more interesting, the boy she was asking about was Brent.

Brent and some of his friends had seen us pinching pennies—that's what we called taking the money from the leprechaun traps that the humans set out. Brent swooped down on Kailee and gave her the 'ol "what'cha doin'." Brent, being the exceptional flyer he is, did this while inverted and flying face-to-face underneath her. Kailee was awed. There was a brief conversation between them before Brent winked and Kailee blushed and Brent darted over to show off to me.

"What'cha' doin'," he said.

"You're in my airspace, fly boy," I replied.

"Whoa, easy there queen bee. I just wanted to say 'Hi'. See how things are going."

"We're doing fine, thanks."

"Almost got one tonight," said Brent.

"One what?" I asked.

41

"A lepe."

"No!"

"Yes!"

"Nuh uh!"

"Uh huh."

"They don't exist," I said.

"Yes they do," replied Brent.

"Maybe in Europe," I said.

"Of course they aren't natural to North America. They came over with Irish immigrants," he explained. "Evil little twerps, I'm telling you."

"Who, the Irish?"

"No, leprechauns, you goof."

"Just wanted to be sure," I smirked. "How close did you get?"

"I don't know about two feet," he said then shouted to his friend. "Rhine, how close did I get to the lepe? About two feet?"

"Sure, whatever," said Rhine.

"I'd say about two feet," Brent confirmed to me. "Almost caught him pinchin' pennies on one of those silly human traps."

"Right," I replied sarcastically. "Is that what you told Kailee?"

Brent grinned, "No. I was just chattin' her up a little. She's cool but she's easily impressed. You, not so much."

"I'm not easily impressed?" I inquired.

"Are you impressed that I almost got a lepe tonight?" he asked.

"No, because they don't exist," I said.

"See," he said.

I rolled my eyes at him. He grinned and raised his eyebrows at me.

"Have fun tonight," he said.

"Bye," I cooed.

Brent rolled one-hundred and eighty degrees to my left and floated toward his friends who were getting away. He got about twenty feet away and yelled back, "Two feet!" then darted off to catch the others.

This was the boy Kailee was asking about. He had changed a lot since the day I tore my dress playing Touch-and-Go the day before kindergarten. But was he cute? I don't know. What is cute? Is cute the color of his hair or his eyes or the size of his nose or mouth? Is cute just his height and weight or does shoulder width play a factor? If it is everything together, do some things take precedence over others? Like are blue eyes enough to offset brown hair when you prefer red? And is cute just looks or do we take into account personality? The one thing I knew was that cute was subjective. No two people thought exactly alike. While there were definitely qualities all girls held in high esteem, there were very few that everyone thought were absolutely bad or couldn't be overlooked if the person had the right personality. So when Kailee asked me if I thought Brent was cute, I considered all his physical elements, his flying ability, his ability to talk with just about anyone, and the fact that he has his own catch phrase. Yeah, I guess he's cute. But instead of telling Kailee what I thought, I turned to Cora and said, "I don't know. Cora, what do you think?" I was smart enough already to know how to avoid the trap that those types of questions can create.

CHAPTER EIGHT

Life's Lessons Turn Hard

Mother was waiting up for me when I wandered in just before midnight. She sat wrapped in a blanket reading a book in the perch we used to share as few as three years ago. Now the perch was too small for both of us and I did most of my reading alone in my room. She looked tired but perked up when I entered. There was so much to talk about that my eem must have been bursting.

"Well?" Mother asked with a smile.

"It was so much fun," I babbled. "Half the fifth grade must have been out tonight. Thank you for letting me go. Darnan dressed up like a leprechaun and knocked on some human's windows. When the humans would look, he flew away along the ground so it looked like he was running. At this one house, the people came running after him. It was so funny."

"What did you do?" asked Mother. "Did you get any money?"

"We pinched a few coins," I answered. "Cora likes to put pennies heads down and see if the humans turn them over to heads up for good luck or if they just pick them up and take them. I'm always surprised at how many people will just leave them on the sidewalk like they aren't worth anything. I got some quarters. I'll probably give them to the tooth fairies or drop a few in front of some deserving kids. Mostly Kailee and Cora and I just flew around and watched the others pull pranks on the humans. Brent and his friends caught up with us and we goofed around a little. Brent said he got within two feet of a leprechaun."

"Ah, Brent," smiled Mother, "he is a bit of a joker, isn't he?"

I paused briefly before asking, "Do you think he's cute?"

"I don't typically look at boys that way but, I guess, all things considered, I would say he is cute," replied Mother. "Do you think he's cute?" she returned.

"I don't know," I said. "I've never looked at boys as anything but trouble. You always said 'boys are trouble.'"

"I guess I don't remember that," added Mother.

"Well, they push you if they like you and tell gross, stupid jokes and typically are just looking out for themselves," I added. "They think girls can't do anything and always pick us last for Touch-and-Go. The only one not afraid to pick me is Brent and that's because he knows

I'm faster than him. I don't know. I guess Brent's not like the other boys. I guess he could be cute. It's all so stupid."

"What brought on all this 'stupidity?'" asked Mother.

"Kailee asked me if I thought Brent was cute tonight," I answered.

"Oh," said Mother as she set her book down on the table. She wrapped the blanket a little more tightly around her shoulders and motioned for me to sit. "You'd better sit down."

"Now what?" I asked.

"It is a little late to be starting a conversation like this but, as you will soon find out, it is important," she began. "First, I will offer my condolences for your loss."

"My loss?" I wondered aloud.

"Yes," said Mother. "You will not be allowed to 'like,' 'have a crush on,' 'swoon over,' or whatever kids your age call it now, your friend Brent."

"Why?"

"Because Kailee likes him," she said matter-of-factly.

"So? Why can't I like someone that she likes?" I asked.

"Because you can't, if you value your reputation and your friendship with Kailee. If those things don't matter to you then you are free to do whatever you like. But, if you, in some real or misconstrued manner, show that you like Brent before Kailee is done liking

47

him, Kailee will think that you have put your desires ahead of your friendship and will be offended and insulted and the rest of the school will label you a 'tramp' or 'slut', or whatever kids your age label tramps and sluts these days, and your whole life will be ruined."

I took a moment to process everything she had said in her very long and confusing run-on sentence, and then protested, "But they are both my friends. I've known Brent longer than I've known Kailee."

"That is true. I would make it a point to remind Kailee of that tomorrow," advised Mother.

"What if Brent doesn't like her?"

"That's a whole other story," said Mother. "One for when it isn't so late or you don't have school the next day. We can talk about the rest of this tomorrow. We should go to bed now."

Mother made her way toward the stairs to her room. I was still flustered. This couldn't be right. Boys couldn't possibly come between me and my friends. Boys and girls are two separate entities and never shall the two meet. I vowed to not let the two mingle within my life and if *I* could keep them apart, Kailee and Cora could too. Right? Nothing to it.

But why did Kailee ask me if I thought Brent was cute? Oh no, they're already mingling. Now what do I do? This is stupid! It's all just stupid and doesn't make any sense and can't possibly be right.

"This is stupid," I blurted out before Mother reached the top of the steps. "You don't know what you're talking about."

"Excuse me?" she replied calmly as she took two steps back down the stairs. "What was that?"

"That may have been the way it was when you were growing up but things are different now," I explained condescendingly.

"Oh, well, then good night," was her simple reply as she turned and continued to bed.

And that was when life's lessons became hard. The moment I said, "You don't know what you're talking about."

Those who fail to learn from history are doomed to repeat it. You know why that is true? It is true because there is only one history and it's repeated in every single generation. The only life lessons that are definite, etched in stone for everyone to learn, are learned during the years from infancy to adulthood, from zero to eighteen or even twenty-two or twenty-five. There is not a story you can share that anyone older than you has not seen, heard, lived, or better yet, survived. Everyone lives through the same stuff and each of us is too stupid to listen to what their parents or grandparents say when they try to help us learn from their mistakes.

It's like when someone tells you that fire burns. Sometime before you are an adult, you will stick your finger into a flame just so you can experience the sensation of burning first hand. I think we do it because we all need a point of reference so when someone later says something will burn, we can ask "Like what? Like a match or a stove?" That way we have an idea of just how badly it will burn as if the fact that it will burn at all isn't enough information. It isn't until adulthood when we have made a comfortable number of these blunders that we begin to take other people's word as proof enough and no longer need to test the flame for heat. But here I was, nearing the end of fifth grade, proclaiming that I knew more than the woman who birthed me. Had I been smart, I would have retracted my statement immediately and apologized for even thinking the thought. Unfortunately for me, Mother knew we had crossed that threshold the moment the words exited my mouth, and, me being the proud eleven-year-old that I was, I went ahead and tossed a match onto the gasoline-soaked metaphorical bridge I had just crossed.

CHAPTER NINE

Supporting the Girls

*S*ome of the biggest changes I would have to endure growing up were physical. My body was changing like crazy. I was becoming a woman. I had new curves where things used to be straight and bumps where things used to be flat. Fortunately we don't have the problem humans do with hair growing out of weird parts of their bodies. That's just gross. My own changes were still going to take some getting used to. Fortunately I had Mother to help me. For Mother, helping meant shopping.

Mother understood middle school better than most parents. She knew that the first thing we needed to do was get hip with the clothing. The "in" look was grungy and ragged so all the clothes were pre-ripped and torn as if I had been wearing them for recess for the last year. I spent the last six years of my life trying desperately to not catch a sleeve or a pant leg on a tree branch and now I was trying on three and four brands of pants and tops that had "designer shredding." This was going to be great!

"I don't understand fashion these days," Mother said somewhat disgusted. "These clothes make you look like a hill-fairy. I could have saved a lot of money by just patching up your Touch-and-Go clothes from last year if you hadn't grown so much."

I had grown from three-and-a-half leafs to a full four leafs in the last year (a leaf is equal to about three human inches). That may not seem like a lot but since I most likely will only grow to be five leafs tall, it was a bunch. Mother cut my long pants into shorts for the summer to save money and found that some of my fancier dresses worked nicely as sun dresses with a couple of alterations. But today my basket runneth over. I had four pair of denim pants, six different tops, and eight T-shirts; Mother hated T-shirts and these were the kind you would tie in a knot at your side to show your midriff. Mother really did not like me showing off my midriff.

"All of this stuff is ridiculous," I heard her grumble as she counted the items in the cart. "It makes you look poor."

"We don't need to buy all of this," I said.

"You need clothes," she replied. "You grew too much last year."

"Where will we get the money for all this?" I asked.

"Don't worry about the money. Do you like them?"

"Yes. It's what everyone will be wearing."

"Okay, then, we only need to get one more thing," she said.

"Mother, this is way more than enough," I said.

"This is something you need. Grab the basket and follow me."

Mother floated through the rest of the teen department stopping only once to say, "You shouldn't need anything like that for awhile," when I held up a low-cut top that showed some cleavage. I kind of wanted something that would show off my newest parts.

Mother navigated her way through the young adult section and the women's department and came to a stop in the underwear aisle. To be more specific, it was the bra aisle. Bras as far as the eye could see. Big bras, little bras, black and white bras. It looked like a Dr. Seuss book about female underwear. There were cotton and silk and hemp and wool. Some were padded and some plain. Some lifted and separated while others minimized. Some had pictures of princesses on them; I assume these were for very young girls who blossomed early or for girls whose mothers didn't want them to grow up. The place was intimidating and I didn't want to be there.

"We aren't stopping here, are we?" I hoped aloud.

"Sweetie," Mother said matter-of-factly, "if you

want them to stay firm and perky, your 'girls' are going to need support. Leave the basket and come with me. Looks like the teen bras are just over here."

She walked deliberately down the aisle of mounded material glancing back toward me, or should I say my chest, whenever she passed something that caught her eye. We weaved through the maze of curved fabric until we reached the back wall which was also closest to the dressing rooms.

There we found almost as many styles and fabrics as the world has dogs all in one cup size: bee sting. Mother selected a simple black one with a trace of lace from the shelf and pushed it against my clothed chest.

"Mother!"

"Really, Rebecca," she said matter-of-factly, "it has to be done. Besides, no one is looking. You know some girls never get out of this cup size."

"Time to bracket the boobs, is it?" blurted a female voice. An older, well-dressed, buxom fairy rounded the corner with a handful of bras that she appeared to be restocking. "Yeah, I remember getting my first bra. My girls hit me like the mumps—fast and furious. Talk about making mountains out of mole hills. I just about had to learn how to fly all over again. That's a terrific every-day piece," she added acknowledging the bra pressed against my chest. "We have a couple more that you might con-sider for more formal occasions and for sports."

"I think we have things under control," Mother stated firmly.

"I understand. My name is Vernal," offered Vernal. "I'll just be flutterin' around here putting these discards away if you need anything."

"Thank you. We'll look for you if we have any questions," answered Mother.

"Oh, look," interjected Vernal as she held out a bra from her stack, "this one is very popular right now. It has the new strap system that goes around the wing rods. They're a little tricky at first but I hear great things about them. This looks like it might be your size."

Then she actually pressed the bra against my chest! She didn't even care that she was pushing on my breasts!

"Mother?!" I pleaded hoping she would say something to this apparent child molester.

"I would appreciate you not being so familiar with my daughter," Mother said properly.

"You should try it on," said Vernal seemingly oblivious to Mother's last statement.

Through the dressing room door I could hear Vernal recommending new bra styles for Mother while I tried to strap the new contraption to the front of my body as fast as possible.

"I think her left one is a little bigger than her right," whispered Vernal to Mother.

"I can't believe you just said that," I hollered through the door.

"Don't worry sweetie," Vernal hollered back. "No one has two that are the same; no one with natural ones anyway."

My hands were not used to this type of contraption and I became flustered. "Mother, I can't get this," I sighed.

"Would you like me to help?" asked Vernal. "They can be tricky to get just right."

"I think I can figure it out," said Mother confidently as she entered the small room.

After a few minutes Mother, too, gave up. Her sigh of frustration must have sounded like a call for help because the door flew open and Vernal's hands suddenly grabbed the front of the bra, pushed my breasts up into the cups and attached the hook in the front.

"How does that feel?" she asked nonchalantly while adjusting the many straps around my shoulders and back. She methodically poked her fingers into the gaps and crevices created by pushing my "girls" up and together and fine tuned the straps she had already adjusted. In a few short minutes, everything felt surprisingly good.

Bras are the only underwear that stores let you try on before you buy it. They are also the only underwear that offers an "expert" to help you decide the correct fit and support. Can you imagine little Johnny going in to buy some briefs to support his 'Little Johnny'? If some "boxer/briefs specialist" came charging into a dressing room poking around between little Johnny's legs, you can bet Johnny's father would have that specialist bloody-nosed and face down on the floor in about two seconds. But here I was with a total stranger's finger between my female parts. A stranger who, at one time, actually asked me, "Did you name them yet?"

I left the underwear department with a shred of dignity and three, cotton, "bee sting" sized bras. I had survived the embarrassment associated with this rite of passage unique to the female gender but I also no longer felt embarrassed or uncomfortable about the changes that were happening to my body. I guess Vernal's crude, unsympathetic, unemotional approach had a purpose after all. Physically, I was becoming a woman; that's just what happens to girls. Everybody does it in different ways and at different times. We all end up with the parts necessary to procreate. It's no big deal. At least it shouldn't be. Of course I threatened to punch Mother in the nose if she ever let Vernal come near me again, to which she just asked, "Don't you have school tomorrow?"

CHAPTER TEN

My Introduction to Evil

*M*iddle School is the place where the colonies take all the most irrational, illogical, ignorant, self-absorbed people they can find and stick them all together in a building for seven hours a day and hope they don't kill each other. The girls are catty and the boys measure themselves by arbitrary ratings of toughness or coolness. Everyone wants to be popular and no one thinks they are. The most anyone can hope for is to fit in with everyone so no one has anything bad to say about you behind your back. If you are lucky you have an inner circle of friends that you can count on no matter what happens to you. I still had Kailee and Cora.

"Not cute. Cute. Cute. Not so cute. Is that one even a fairy?" was what Kailee considered conversation when she, Cora and I flew into the mass of twelve- and thirteen-year-old fairies in front of Madelyn Middle School. Kailee and Cora were no more boy crazy than any other girl our age. The boys weren't much different with their new feelings toward the opposite sex, they just didn't know what to do with them. All of this craziness was the result of the changes taking place in everyone's bodies.

It used to be that kids were short or tall, fat or thin, or just average. Now, bone and muscle structure were becoming more pronounced. Shoulders and backs began to broaden and hips and butts took form. Legs and arms got longer and more or less muscular. For girls, it was the breasts. Having gone through what I just did in the bra department, I didn't think much about them until today and the way some of them were on display. "Really?" I said as a well-endowed eighth-grader fluttered past wearing a low-cut top.

"It's the only way anyone will talk to her," said Cora.

"Hey, I have that top," defended Kailee.

"Not that chest," I said.

"But you also have a personality," said Cora.

Kailee, Cora, and I had very few classes together. The lack of a classroom for everyone to call home created the need for groups where like-minded individuals could feel comfortable. You might know them as cliques. Middle school was full of cliques. There were the athletes— mostly the flying team—builders/ thatchers, artists, geeks, nerds and the populars.

Within any of these groups would be a blend of males and females, except for the flying team. Girl's are not allowed on the Touch-and-Go team until high school because "we are too fragile," so I was told. Unlike humans, female fairies are smaller than the males when we are younger but become much stronger after transition which I think you humans call puberty. The clique hierarchy was something that only the very few who were truly comfortable with themselves could avoid. I had no intention of falling, or being placed, into it.

There was this one group of girls who didn't fit into any of the more established stereotypes. They weren't really popular but hung out around the fringe of the popular kids' circle waiting for a moment when they would be included for a day or two. They were just sort of average at pretty much everything except one: making others unhappy. They were The Evils.

I think it is funny how evil geniuses are usually portrayed as males. Women and girls are much more creative when it comes to destroying people than men and boys. Males are blatant and crude while females are subtle and sneaky. Males are like the blast from the atomic bomb while females are the nuclear fallout that does the subtle, permanent damage. One of these nuclear moves involved snickering amongst themselves as they glared at the intended target. The glare could be done across a hallway or cafeteria or while passing the victim.

The truly talented could do this and make their presence known behind the target's back, adding insult to injury by turning a metaphor into a literal action. And nobody was safe. I have even seen these people turn on their own by conveniently ignoring a friend during class or leaving someone behind if they should drop something on the way into the school. All of this is done to create insecurity and self-doubt in kids who had no shortage of that to begin with.

Since the Evils never really cared about anyone other than themselves, it was difficult to connect with their eems to better understand them. I still wonder why these girls are this way. Were they denied attention at home or were they the center of attention at home but not at school? Were they the children of unhappy marriages or did they come from single-parent homes like me? Were their families spiritual or mythologists, large or small, rich or poor, fat or thin? The truth is that these girls came from all types of families. The only thing they had in common was a need to make themselves feel better by making someone else feel worse. That satisfaction was, at best, fleeting because they still had to look in the mirror that night or the next morning and everything they didn't like about themselves was still going to be staring right back at them. That is why they needed a target every day.

The Evils—Kendra, Shelby and Taylor—were psycho killers who would use subtle forms of torture to make other kids go crazy. Their most popular method of manipulation was spreading lies about someone through their network of gossips. The lies would be so subtle that everyone who heard them would just assume they were true. By the time the lie reached the person it was about, it was almost impossible to get the truth out and the victim would usually not bother trying to change things. But there was one thing the Evils liked better than a good lie to spread and that was a damning truth. Everybody has one. I wondered what was the deep, dark secret that would destroy each of them? Unfortunately, they had no deep, dark secrets. They shared everything with everyone; especially the dark moments of their lives. They thrived on the attention and sympathy that having lived through such anguish afforded them. If anything, they tended to exaggerate the truth to make themselves even more pitiful.

In elementary school it was widely known that my father had "died tragically in an autumn leaf-coloring accident." That is what Mother had decided to go with after trying out a number of different stories on her boyfriends and our neighbors. It is also what she had told me for the previous twelve years. The more I thought about it, the more I knew that this version of my past would not be exposed by The Evils. All three of these girls had both of their parents even though some of them were pretty pathetic. My having lost my father before I was born would only bring me greater sympathy from the rest of the school. There would be no benefit to The Evils from exposing it unless they found the truth that I was the bastard child of Michelle DuVall and some unknown guy.

I would sometimes envision what my father looked like. I pictured him as tall, but not too tall, maybe six or seven leaves, strong without being burly, smart and gentle without being afraid to wrestle with me. I saw him teaching me the secrets of the forests and streams and holding me in his arms as we flew across the treetops during a clear, full-moon night. When we were done, I would fall asleep on his chest with his arms wrapped around me as a gentle breeze swung us back and forth in a hammock. He was as perfect as an imaginary father could be. But my father was dead, in essence anyway. In fact, who really knew? But for the first time I was angry that he was not there for me.

CHAPTER ELEVEN

Dating from a Distance

I was half way through grade seven. Boys had girlfriends and girls had boyfriends and I just laughed at all of them. How silly were these "couples" that lasted for a day or a week or, if you were very lucky, a month. Cora's experiences were few but typically fell into the longer lasting category. I don't know if it was because she was more selective or because she was more patient with her boyfriends.

Kailee, on the other hand, seemed to be cycling through the entire seventh grade. We calculated that she averaged one boy per week. She'd be asked to "go out" by someone on Monday, spend around two days holding hands and, on rare occasions, would actually kiss him in public. She would have an emotional disagreement with him on day three or four followed by a break up on day five leaving her so distraught that it seemed as if she had just lost the love of her life. The schedule was consistent and accurate to within two days.

Cora and I played along with the drama. We would console Kailee and huddle in her room while she cried. I never understood how she could cry that much over each of these guys. There were so many ex-boyfriends that even the boys started to think it was a joke. It became a game to see which boy would be the last to be Kailee's boyfriend. They had rules and everything.

Rule #1; no asking her out while she is going out with someone else. The flood of proposals immediately following a break-up (the number diminishing by one after each relationship) helped Kailee bounce back quicker and even started to make her a little cocky. After all, she was the most popular girl in seventh grade, wasn't she?

Rule #2; you may not go out with Kailee more than once. This was to ensure that the other boys would get a chance. The "most times dating Kailee" contest would come after the current competition was over.

Rule #3; no kissing on the lips. I didn't quite get this one. Maybe it had something to do with kissing-transmitted diseases.

No one wanted to be last. Even the geeks started vying for her attention at lunch time with hopes of not being labeled "Kailee's Last Man." We didn't know what was going on until the end of the school year when Jarfer and Durnam, the school's biggest geeks, kept sending Kailee fruit and nut baskets. Of course Kailee was devastated when she found out and swore off boys for the rest of her life. That lasted about two weeks although she didn't date anyone for a whole month. I sometimes think the whole thing was just a game to Kailee too. I think, somewhere in the back of her mind, she was also keeping score and would have liked to have gotten those last two notches in her belt but had to put on the appropriate show for us to cover up for all the other distress caused by the previous break-ups. All I know is that as the boyfriend casualty numbers grew, the pain in Kailee's eem seemed to be less and less intense.

I was not as fortunate as my friends at the art of dating and boyfriends. I don't know why. Maybe it was because I was in that awkward time of my life where I didn't feel pretty. Maybe it was because I was an intim-idating athlete or because I was a very good student. Maybe it was because I was holding a grudge against my absent father so I spent my time finding faults in each boy instead of looking for positive characteristics. Maybe it was because I didn't feel I needed someone else to make me feel complete. Maybe it was a combi-nation of all of these things. Whatever it was that kept me from getting close to the opposite sex, I was ready to be done with it.

I wondered how I would feel having a boy hold my hand or having him give me a hug or even, in the right moment, a kiss. I remembered watching Mother flirt with her boyfriends but didn't want to just use boys the way she used those men. I felt the eem from too many of Kailee's stories to count, but feeling someone else's eem is not the same as doing it yourself. And who's to say that I would have the same feelings? I wanted a boyfriend. Someone who wanted to be together for awhile and not just hug and kiss and hold hands for a week and then try it again with someone else.

But who? I spent one lunch period just looking at the options and trying to focus on the good features of each. "They all seem so immature," I thought. Oops, not a good start. I refocused my energy and began the weeding out process. The first boy to get my attention, Burl, did so by dumping nectar down the back of a girl named Autumn and laughing. He was out. Then came Clark, who is nice but so simple that I was never able to have a conversation with him of any real length or depth or interest. Marnil, very nice and smart but not very cute (cute is important); Darvin, too young and a nerd. After one whole lunch period evaluating boys, I was left with about five marginal options and one of those was Brent who was already going out with Breezy.

Maybe next year.

CHAPTER TWELVE

So This is How it Starts

Grade eight brought lots of changes. Mostly I spent a lot of time alone. Kailee used the summer break to fix her image. She no longer *needed* to have a boyfriend which made the relationships she sought last longer. She also spent more time getting to know the boy before accepting the invitation to "go out" or "go steady" or whatever you call it these days.

Cora's dad gave up trying to save his old business and took a job as a woodland fairy on the other side of the valley. He had been the primary caregiver in the family but now was gone for weeks at a time. Since her mom always worked a lot, Cora was stuck watching her little brother after school and wasn't able to hang out very much. To top it all off, Kailee and Cora had a different lunch period than me and I didn't feel ready to seek out a new group to sit with.

I'd built a reputation as someone who got along with

almost anybody. It came mostly from being willing to have a conversation with anyone who spoke to me first. I found that a simple "how are you doing?" and caring enough to wait for the answer was all it took to be considered a decent person.

But that particular day I wasn't looking for company and chose a seat toward the rear of the tree where my back faced the trunk. The whole tree lay before me. It was the safest place to be if you didn't want anyone talking behind your back. So I was sitting by myself in one of the two safest seats in the place when I heard the familiar song styling of Brent singing, "what'cha doin' Rebecca?" coming from the side.

"Hi Brent," I answered.

"Mind if we join you?" he asked. Brent had brought his crew which included Rhine, Azure and Train. The four made up half of the school Touch-and-Go team last year. Three of them knew I could kick their butts. Rhine had gotten a lot bigger over the summer. He might be a little tougher to beat now. Either way, I was suddenly sitting with the Jocks and the eyes of the Populars and the Evils were upon me.

"I'd really rather sit by myself," I said. "I don't need everyone looking at me."

"Too late," said Brent casually, "they're already looking and if they see us walk away, you'll be labeled 'the girl who got shunned by the Jocks.' Now, I don't want that. And I don't think Rhine wants that, do you Rhine?"

"No, I don't want that," said Rhine in a sincere and sympathetic tone.

There was a silent pause as he and I glanced at each other's faces then looked down at our lunches. He looked a lot different than I remembered. Not only was he bigger but his facial features were more defined, his voice was lower and he seemed, I don't know, shy. He wanted to be there with me but he seemed embarrassed about it. He would glance up at me then quickly turn toward Brent or look to his food. He just seemed so sweet and innocent and so cute! I just wanted to wrap him up in my arms like a little puppy dog and kiss his little nose and scratch him behind the ears. Suddenly I felt happy and scared and nervous and uncertain and I didn't know what I was supposed to do but I knew nothing good would come from them leaving so I said shyly, "I don't want that either."

"Then we will stay," said Brent and he went on eating and talking about the new school year and the Touch-and-Go season and other stuff I barely heard. I didn't eat my lunch for fear of looking weird in front of Rhine. I needed to see what I looked like while chewing before I could ever eat in front of him. I could wait until dinner for nourishment. I don't remember him eating much either but who really knows. When Brent and the others finished, they gathered their trash and rose to leave.

"I think this went well. Same place tomorrow?" asked Brent. Rhine just looked at me.

"Sure," I said.

"Cool," said Brent as they turned away. Brent stopped quickly and turned back. "Hey, Rebecca, you coming to the flying team tryouts tonight?"

"They don't have a girl's team," I said.

"Maybe you could change their minds," said Azure.

"Careful, dude, she can take you," said Rhine.

"It would be over in a blink," added Brent.

"I don't know. I'll see," I answered.

"It starts at three. All the cool kids will be there," said Brent.

"Not if I'm not there," I added.

"Very true," he agreed.

I waited for Kailee and Cora after school to tell them about my lunch experience. They were suprised. I guess I was too. We had known Rhine for a couple years now. He and Brent hung out together from about fourth grade on and were always on the same Touch-and-Go team when we played twos. He was always a little bigger than Brent and didn't say much but he was nice. He didn't talk down to girls and never did immature stuff like pushing or punching or pulling hair if he liked you. I don't know if he even liked girls that much until this year.

"Oh, my, Gods!" squealed Kailee. "Really, you and Rhine?"

"He is *so* cute this year," said Cora.

"He didn't ask me out or anything," I answered. "He was just nice to me."

"But he looked into your eyes," said Cora. "You said he looked into your eyes."

"Is that such a big deal?" I asked. "Eye contact is a common courtesy when talking to someone."

"We have to go to the tryouts," squealed Kailee.

"We do," added Cora. "We absolutely have to go."

"Why would that make a difference? And why would I want to torture myself with being near the Touch-and-Go field?"

"You have to go," said Kailee. "They invited you. You were asked to be there."

"We know who will make the team," I said. "It's the same six or seven every year with one or two exceptions."

"They just want to show off," said Cora. "That's what the male of the species does."

"Let them have their moment in the sun," added Kailee. "Rhine wants you there."

"Okay, okay," I said reluctantly, "I'll go."

CHAPTER THIRTEEN

Boyfriend, What a Concept

*K*ailee, Cora and I arrived at the Touch-and-Go field at three o'clock exactly so we wouldn't distract any of the team—unlike the other girls in our class who flirted with and fawned over the boys as they stretched and warmed up. How pathetic.

The field was the same one the high school used and it was amazing. The leaves had bold and beautiful colors. The new growth on the primary branches was trimmed back while the more radical outer foliage was left to fill in creating new hazards. The time-tested routes used by the star players of the past remained but there were some great new paths to be carved by someone with a creative mind and the guts to go for it. Next year I would get to fly on this field.

The boys finished their warm-ups by practicing rolls and dives. Brent did his signature "backstroke" move which is what he named his inverted flying maneuver. He zoomed past the crowd of mostly seventh and eighth grade girls and hollered "what'cha doin'." The crowd cheered for the team captain. Kailee and Cora dragged me closer to the mob so we could get a better view of the safe spot which is where the more dramatic action takes place. I couldn't believe I was here.

I could see Rhine across the field flying faster than he ever had but he was a little clumsy as a result of his new growth. He would be okay. His size made him a good blocker and his speed might get him some time at the sprint position in the more open fields he would see when we played teams further from the mountains. The glamour positions are the sprinters and weavers like Brent. Weavers tend to be smaller flyers that can maneuver through tight spots. They usually were limited to short bursts of speed and didn't do well in an open sprint. Brent and I were the exceptions.

The coach called everyone in and lined them up by height. They all had to hover in place while he shouted out directions. The hovering was part of conditioning. Rhine and Brent were on opposite ends of the line with eight others in between. They had not been this far apart for as long as I could remember. Rhine looked behind the row of flyers toward Brent and saw me sitting on a perch at the edge of the crowd. He smiled and winked and I smiled and blushed. "Rhine, let's go," yelled the coach to his distracted athlete. Rhine darted off to catch the others who had started flying laps.

The boys made ten trips around the fifty-yard-square field following Brent through the easiest path he could find. It was more a warm-up than anything. The buzzing of the wings grew and decreased as they neared and got further away. The drills continued on with weaving exercises, sprint timing, climbing and diving drills and finally an actual game. The only way to truly test someone's talent is to get them into a game.

The two teams of five players huddled along the sidelines. Brent and Rhine were on separate teams. It was up to them to decide which strategies and techniques they would use—who they would go after first and how they would catch them? Would they use a blocker or do a squeeze play or just a fly-by or simply choose more dramatic paths that only the best weavers could navigate? The game changed constantly but most dramatically when a player was caught. It all came down to proper placement and communication.

The teams broke their huddles and spread out across the field. Brent and Rhine went in opposite directions as was expected. The best players prefer to have the field to themselves so no one else gets in the way of their dash to the safe spot. Unless something went wrong, it would come down to Brent and Rhine. The game started with Dargon making a typically bad attempt to make a name for himself by going after the best player on the other team. Rhine took the tag with a smile and quickly darted toward Dargon. Just as Rhine was about to make the pass, Moss and Clay collapsed on him from both sides squeezing against his body and slowing his progress allowing Dargon to beat him to the safe spot. Rhine was caught and, with Brent still out there, it didn't look good for his teammates getting him free.

"Well that was stupid," said Kailee.

"Shh," I warned.

"Even I know not to get tagged in the beginning of the game," she added. "There are too many players out there to get in your way."

"I'm sure he knows that," said Cora.

"I'm just sayin'," added Kailee.

"Shh," I warned again. "Someone might hear you."

The game ended quickly with Brent's team catching the rest of Rhine's team in less than five minutes. It was the shortest Touch-and-Go game I can remember. The tryouts were over. Brent and the other boys were mobbed by the crowd of girls that had watched the festivities. Rhine pulled himself away from the crowd and fluttered toward me, Kailee and Cora.

"Here comes Rhine. We'd better go," said Kailee.

"Good luck on the tryouts," she said to Rhine as they passed each other.

"See you later," Cora said to me as they floated away.

Rhine and I watched my friends float out of sight then he turned to me and said, "Pretty stupid, huh?"

"What? Getting caught?" I asked.

"Yeah," he said.

"Yeah, that was pretty dumb," I said. "The game was over after they got you." Rhine just hovered silently for a few seconds. The silence made me uncomfortable. I wondered if I had said something wrong or if he was just nervous. I needed to say something to break the silence. "I don't think it will hurt your chances of making the team. Everyone knows how good you are. You just had an off day."

"Yeah," he said with a hint of a smile. "I just had an off day. I guess I was a little distracted." He smiled impishly at me. I blushed. Things were back to normal. "You want to go for a fly around the field?" he offered.

Rhine and I wandered through the Touch-and-Go field scouting the new growth and looking for more direct routes to the safe spot from different angles. We flew high and low, through the dense outer growth, and between the familiar large branches of the great Cottonwood. Finally we ended up on the edge of the field where we had started.

"I've never had a team run a set on me before," said Rhine. "It felt kind of nice to think that I was nice enough that they wouldn't just go head-to-head against me."

"You deserve that kind of respect," I added, "you're really good. Not as good as me…" I teased.

"Oh, really?" he laughed. "I got a lot stronger over the summer."

"And a little clumsier."

"Clumsier?! Alright, I see where this is going."

"What's that supposed to mean?" I asked. Then Rhine looked at me with a big grin and touched me on the top of my head.

"You have been touched," he said.

"You aren't serious," I challenged.

"Yes, I am," he grinned.

"You really want to do this?" I asked.

"I do."

"You're sure?" I confirmed.

"Absolutely," he confirmed.

"Okay," I said.

"Whenever you're ready," he said.

"On your touch," I said and prepared myself for a race. Rhine rubbed his hands together, extended is index finger and said "Touch" as he poked my shoulder.

Like two rockets, we shot across the open field headed toward the safe spot. We were side-by-side as we approached the more dense growth of the Aspens. There was a hole in the trees large enough for me but would be a tight squeeze for Rhine. I was going for it.

Rhine slid in behind me so we hit the hole single-file. It was over. I knew there was no way he would catch me if I got a full length ahead. We weaved through the Aspens at a reasonable pace since he wasn't going to pass me in the mesh of small branches and emerged on the other side with only a final sprint to the safe spot. It was going to be easy—turn on the jets and leave him in a cloud of leaves. Then he cheated.

I guess he didn't really cheat, per se, because he didn't grab my leg or push me. He didn't throw anything at me or insult me, which isn't illegal anyway. But he did something that made me stop in mid-air. Just before I shifted into overdrive, Rhine yelled, "Will you go out with me?"

I wasn't ready for it. I mean, who asks someone out when they're in the middle of a race? I guess it could happen like that, since, after all, it did. I wouldn't have been fazed by anything else but this was the first time I had been asked out and, well, like I said, I stopped in mid-air and watched him sail past me to the safe spot. I got my bearings and sprinted to the spot in the great Cottonwood where he fluttered catching his breath. My competitive impulses were still in control.

"You didn't win!" I shouted.

"Why not?" he asked.

"You cheated."

"How did I cheat?"

"You yelled that thing at me."

"There's no rule that says you can't yell things," he defended.

"But it's what you yelled."

"What did I yell?"

"You yelled…" I was scared to say what I thought he said. What if he didn't actually say those words? What if it was just the wind howling in my ears? What if it was just my imagination or wishful thinking? Did I actually like a boy enough that I would want him to ask me out?

"What did I yell?" he pressured.

"Nothing," I said. I couldn't take the chance of being wrong and looking like a fool. "You didn't win," I continued sternly. I was flustered and just wanted to leave. If he didn't say what I thought he said then nothing good could come from anything that happened next. Feeling something between embarrassed, anxious and afraid, I said, "I have to go home," and turned to leave.

"So, will you go out with me?" he hollered.

All of my insecurity vanished in an instant and I spun around and shouted, "You did yell that!"

"It's not cheating," he laughed.

"It should be," I proclaimed, "especially if you don't mean it."

"Who says I didn't mean it?" he added.

I again stopped in mid-air. "Are you asking me out?" I asked with a surprised calmness.

"Yes," he said.

"Oh," I replied as I hovered above the Cottonwood branches. Now I had to rethink everything. Inside, my heart was racing and cheering and I felt like flying to the moon. Someone really liked me or maybe even loved me. I know the love thing was a little extreme but it is what I thought. At the same time my brain was spinning with questions of 'do I like him?' and 'what kind of commitment are we talking about here?' Thankfully, my face and body did not reveal the contradictions my heart was experiencing. I think this made him uneasy.

"I wanted to do it at lunch but was too nervous," he said. "I guess I wasn't nervous when we were racing."

'That makes sense,' I thought. In the heat of battle, inhibitions tend to get tossed by the wayside. But is that the only time he feels comfortable around me? I guess we did spend the last hour together alone. I wonder how he is in math because I could use some help in math sometimes. Then I stopped and thought, 'are you crazy? There is a cute, nice boy over there who wants to call you his girlfriend!' I turned around to see Rhine's anxious face and said, "Yes." After a few moments of silence I followed it with, "Now what do we do?"

The Reconnection

Rhine flew me home. We held hands and talked about things we liked and people we didn't. When he dropped me off, we gave each other a hug because we weren't quite ready to try kissing. He waited on the branch outside my door until I got inside then fluttered toward his home turning around once to wave to me as I looked out the window. I think I glided across the floor toward my room.

"Rebecca?" called Mother from the kitchen.

"Yes?" I sang as I collapsed on my bed. The singing got Mother's attention. A moment later she appeared in the doorway.

"You sound very happy," smiled Mother.

"I'm okay," I said not really wanting to talk about my day. Mother was not excited about me having a boyfriend however inevitable it may have been. But it's a parent's responsibility to know what is going on in their child's life so she began her typical parental interrogation. It always starts with a simple question.

"Just okay?" she said.

"Maybe even pretty good," I answered slyly.

"Were did you go after school?" she asked simply.

Now I knew that if I said 'I went to the Touch-and-Go team tryouts,' she would ask 'with whom?' and I would answer 'with Kailee and Cora' and she would wonder 'why?' because none of us go to the games because we don't get to play (not that Kailee or Cora like playing as much as me anyway). Mother then would ask 'did you go to see Brent?' because she knows we are friends to which I could say 'yes' because he, technically, is the person who invited me, to which she would then ask 'do you like him?,' and I would say 'he's nice for a boy,' and she would say 'yes he is' and the conversation would be over. This sounded good to me. I wouldn't have to lie and say something like 'I stayed after to work on math' which never, ever works, and I didn't have to tell her about Rhine because she didn't ask. So I went all-in with the partial truth.

"I went to the Touch-and-Go team tryouts with Kailee and Cora," I said.

"How did Rhine do?" Mother asked.

Where did that come from?! How could she know?! Where do adults come up with this stuff?! Do they have eyes in the backs of their heads? Do they

have spies everywhere? Maybe they're all linked tele-
pathically.

"I saw you two holding hands as you flew up," she
said. "He grew quite a bit over the summer."

Oh great. Now she knows I have a boyfriend.
Terrific! Now I'll have to listen to her talk about how
boys are nothing but trouble. How they will keep you
from being as smart as you can be and try to make you
wait on them hand and foot. How they think they are
the most important things in the world and they should
each have their own sun that revolves around them. I
really didn't want to hear any of that today. The
boyfriend thing was so new and wonderful and it was
all I wanted to feel and think about and experience at
that time. I didn't need Mother ruining it for me. Again
she surprised me.

"I am happy for you," she said and added "I'm here
if you want to share," then left to finish making dinner.

Mother ate dinner to the sound of my voice telling
the story of how the entire day transpired. So much had
happened in such a short amount of time: the first day
of school, eating lunch without Kailee and Cora for the
first time, having the Jocks sit with me and invite me to
tryouts, and being asked out by Rhine.

It had been a while since Kailee and Cora were not
the first to hear about a major experience. Had I cared
enough to notice, I would have seen the big smile on

Mother's face confirming that my eem was very strong with her again and that our renewed connection made her happy. But I just kept blabbering on and on and finally ended with, "Can I go to Kailee's?"

Her smile faded and she looked down at her plate. She wanted to say something but was doing her best to not rain on my parade.

"I don't have any homework and I'll do the dishes before I go," I added.

She forced a smile and said, "I will do the dishes. I know this is a big day for you. Go to Kailee's."

I thanked her, kissed her on the cheek and left her alone with the dishes. At a time when we connected stronger than we had for two years, I chose to leave her alone. And she, against her own wishes and desires, allowed me to go. Had she not let me go, I probably would have accused her of being selfish and unfair and stormed off to my room and slammed the door or some other immature and selfish thing. If she mentioned wanting to talk with me I probably would have assumed she was going to be warning me to be careful or to not take things too seriously. In the short amount of time it took for her to look into a dish and sigh, she anticipated all of that and chose to be alone with the dishes over alone with a disgruntled daughter locked in a bedroom. Wow.

CHAPTER FIFTEEN

Is it Really That Big a Deal?

ow could news travel so fast? Why would anyone even care? Boys I barely knew were coming up to me and telling me how stupid I was to go out with Rhine. They called him a wimp and a dumb Jock. One person asked me if I knew what he did last year then never told me what it was when I asked. One said Rhine had gotten mad and choked his last girlfriend.

I also found myself surrounded by some of the popular girls who flew uncomfortably close to me and asked way too many personal questions. They wanted to know all the details of how he asked me out and if he kissed me. I found myself escorted from class to class by one or more of these parasites who served as shields from the other kids. A human might equate it to being a movie star with a security detail. The deftness of their one-handed sweep to clear the others from my path and effectiveness of their "she can't talk now" statement was impressive, to say the least. The only time I was allowed to even make eye contact with anyone was when I saw Rhine approaching from the other direction with his own entourage. In his case, the boys followed behind him in a small cluster as if to wallow in his wake. Only Brent was allowed to walk beside Rhine. Brent said his usual "what'cha doin'?" and Rhine just said "Hey," to which my security detail swooned. I just smiled shyly and said, "Hi." It was crazy. I just hoped to make it to lunch.

I made it through the lunch line without too much effort and headed back to the empty branch where everything started the day before. I positioned myself on the same perch and looked out to the crowd of schoolmates who all seemed to be looking at me and waiting for something to happen. I sat down and twisted the stem from my peach glancing up occasionally to see if the eyes were still on me. Finally I heard the sound of familiar voices.

"Hey Rebecca, what'cha' doin'?" said Brent as he plopped into the perch across from me.

"Hi," said Rhine as he sat down beside me.

"Mind if we sit here?" said Brent. "You don't want to be snubbed by the Jocks."

"Did you all make the team?" I asked Rhine.

"Yep," said Rhine.

"Even after that bonehead move in the tryouts," joked Brent. "First one caught and he makes the team. I guess they lowered the standards this year."

"You set me up," said Rhine to Brent.

"You can't prove that," said Brent.

"Clay, Moss and Dargon all said you set the play up," said Rhine.

"Yeah, well, who believes them anyway?" countered Brent.

I looked out over the now less-interested crowd. I guess everyone had their proof now that Rhine and I were going out. The Populars would still glance in our direction on occasion and turn to each other and giggle. The builders and nerds didn't bother looking anymore. But one person seemed especially focused on our table: Shelby.

"How's your day been?" asked Rhine.

"Crazy," I said. "How about you?"

"Nuts," he replied. "I see you have some new friends."

"I'm sure it's temporary," I scoffed. They just want the inside scoop. I see you have some new fans."

"Those guys will follow anyone with a girlfriend," said Rhine.

"I wish Kailee and Cora didn't have late lunch," I said.

"Hey, you got us," said Brent.

Things quickly quieted down. In two days the Populars decided it was safe for me to walk alone in the halls again and Rhine no longer served as the wedge for his group of followers. Rhine and I would eat lunch a couple branches down from Brent and the Jocks and talk after school before he had practice. After a week no one seemed to care anymore that we were together. Even Kailee and Cora seemed to be okay with waiting a couple extra minutes after school for me. Kailee kind of owed it to me after what Cora and I put up with the previous year. Cora was still watching her brother after school a lot and I was glad she spent what little free time she did have with us. The person that seemed to be the most enthralled with me and Rhine continued to be Shelby. It made me nervous.

"What's up with Shelby?" I asked Kailee and Cora after school.

"I don't know. Why, is she bothering you?" asked Kailee.

"She keeps looking at me and Rhine," I said. "Janny said she keeps asking people about us."

"I don't trust her," said Cora. "She's evil."

"They're all evil," said Kailee, "Her, Taylor, Kendra."

"Why do they want to mess with me?" I asked.

"Girl, they mess with anyone who might be happy," said Kailee.

"They can't hurt you if you don't let them," said Cora.

"Tell me that when she starts watching you all the time," I said.

"So, you're coming up on one week," Kailee said changing the subject. "You gonna kiss him?"

"That's a personal question," defended Cora, "unless you are going to kiss him."

"Well?" said Kailee.

"I don't know," I replied.

"What's the matter, not feeling it?" asked Cora.

"How do you know when you're feeling it?" I asked.

"You don't have to be feeling anything for your first kiss," said Kailee.

"The first kiss is special," gasped Cora. "Don't listen to her."

"Special?!" said Kailee followed by a raspberry. "Just do it and get it out of the way."

"You're joking, right?" said Cora.

"Why would I be joking?" answered Kailee.

"I am so not eeming that. But fine, if you want to be that way," said Cora. "I'm sure *you* don't care any more seeing as how you dated almost the whole seventh grade last year. Don't you remember the pain and anguish you felt every time you broke up with someone? I remember when Brent broke up with you,

you cried for two days and kept saying 'I wasted my first kiss on him.' You lie when you say it isn't special. Stop lying."

"Okay, I'm lying," admitted Kailee. "I was just trying to take the pressure off her." She turned to me, "Look, don't sweat the kiss thing. It's no big deal. Once you do it, you'll wonder what all the fuss was about."

But still, it was going to be my "first kiss". The first one of anything has a level of special to it. I don't care if it's the first strawberry you eat, the first time you fly untethered to your parents, or the first time you hold hands with a boy. This very important event would, at the very least, be a milestone in my life. What would it take to make it special? That's easy, special is the combination of the perfect person, the perfect place, and the perfect time. I knew the perfect place and time—Paris in the spring—but the person was still a mystery. Actually, the place and time were kind of uncertain too since I wasn't going to Paris anytime soon and spring was half a year away. I guess I was going to have to take the whole thing as it came. It would be spontaneous.

"So," started Cora, "are you gonna kiss him?"

"I don't know," I said. "I guess we'll have to just see what happens."

"That's enough talk of kissing already," interrupted Kailee. "I'm hungry. Let's get something to eat."

CHAPTER SIXTEEN

What's In a Nickname

The next day I saw Rhine with Shelby walking to class. Shelby was flirting heavily but I could tell it was all for naught when he stopped in the middle of the hall, and their conversation, to ask how I was doing and give me a hug. Shelby looked annoyed and angry that she was being put off by my boyfriend. Good. I could see her devious mind working behind her squinted eyes. I just smiled at her over Rhine's shoulder as we hugged.

"See you after school?" I asked.

"You got it Becky," said Rhine as he released me.

"What?" I asked.

"Yeah, after school, at the tree," he answered.

"No, what did you call me?" I inquired.

"Becky," he said. "It's short for…"

"I know what it's short for," I said and looked at him in disbelief.

"What's wrong?" he asked.

I saw Shelby's expression transform from anger to delight at the sight of my discomfort. "Nothing," I said flatly and moved briskly down the hall.

No one had ever called me anything but Rebecca, Mother had made sure of that. But here was my first boyfriend trying to create his own pet name and it turns into one of the three derivations I've been fighting all my life. I wished he had called me Snookems or Peaches or anything other than a shorter version of Rebecca. I suddenly realized that, until then, Rhine had never really used my name at all. He would say "Hey" or "Hey you" when we passed or when he would sit with me at lunch but never say, "Hi Rebecca." I didn't know what to do. I could just let it go and see if I liked it. I remembered liking Becky when I was little but I wasn't that into it anymore. My friend's names were Cora, which was short for Coraline, and Kailee, which wasn't short for anything. Rhine's friends had just started calling him Rhino because he had grown so much. He seemed to not mind it although I didn't know if he liked it. And what if he really wanted to call me Becky? What if it was a deal breaker for me to tell him how I felt?

That was how the rest of my day went. With no friends to bounce ideas off of until after school, I was stuck with my thoughts, my concerns and my insecurities for another three hours. I almost got sick. How stupid is that; getting sick over a boy calling you a nickname? The school bell rang and I darted out of my home room and got to Kailee's class before she got out the door.

"Kailee, Kailee," I paged her over the rest of the class.

"What?" she said when she finally got out the door. I dragged her into a corner in the hallway.

"Rhine called me Becky," I said. "What do I do?"

"He called you Becky?"

"Yes. What do I do?"

"Why?"

"Why what?"

"Why did he call you Becky?"

"I don't know. He did it in the hall between third and fourth period. What do I do?"

"I don't know," she said, "do you like being called Becky?"

"After three hours of thinking about it, I'm pretty sure I don't."

"What do you mean 'you're pretty sure'?"

"I don't know," I whined. "Maybe I'll like it more if he says it."

"That could make a difference," said Kailee. Suddenly Cora was next to us.

"What are you doing over here?" Cora asked.

"Rhine called her Becky," said Kailee.

"Really?" asked Cora as she looked at me with astonishment. "What are you going to do?"

"I don't know." I said. "It was a surprise. I don't know if I handled it very well either."

"What did you do?" asked Kailee. "You didn't hit him, did you?"

"No, I didn't hit him! That would be stupid and I'd get suspended."

"What did you do?" asked Cora.

"I just flew away," I answered.

"That doesn't sound so bad," said Cora.

"He was trying to talk to me when I left," I said.

"Oh," said Kailee, acknowledging the faux pas with the tone of the simple utterance.

"He's waiting for me at the tree after school," I added.

"Oh, then, no big deal," said Cora. "Talk to him about it after school. Tell him you don't want to be called Becky. You don't want to be called Becky, do you? I mean, we don't get to call you Becky and we're your best friends."

"You two have called me much worse," I interjected.

"But we do it with love and only the best intentions," said Kailee patronizingly.

"And we are your best friends," added Cora.

"You're right," I said with false confidence. "I'll just tell him I don't like it."

"Okay," said Cora with an air of uncertainty.

"What's the worst thing that could happen?" added Kailee.

"He could dump me," I said.

"I was thinking he could choke you," said Cora.

"Is that true?" I asked astonished.

"No, that's not true," said Kailee, "stop scaring her."

"I don't really think it's true," added Cora. "I don't know why I said it."

"So he might dump you, who cares?" said Kailee. "There are plenty of fairies in the trees. Besides, you still have us."

"Let's hope it doesn't come to that," I said.

"Or choking," added Cora which drew a punch in the arm from Kailee to which Cora modified her statement with, "Which we think is just a rumor."

"I'd better go," I said as I slowly fluttered away. "He's probably waiting for me."

"Tell us how it goes," said Kailee.

I flew to my locker and dropped off my books. I was late. I didn't see Rhine as I usually did—most likely because I had messed up my routine by darting across the school to talk with Kailee and Cora. But I did see Brent.

"Brent," I called as I grabbed his arm.

"Hey Rebecca, what'cha doin'?" he asked.

"Rhine called me Becky today."

"Really?"

"Did you tell him to call me that?" I asked.

"Are you kidding?" he defended, "your mom would kill me if I called you Becky. You want me to tell him to stop?"

"No, thanks. Gotta go, Bye."

I flew out the to giant Cottonwood tree at the center of the Touch-and-Go field where we hung out after school even though the administration preferred we not loiter on school grounds. Rhine was waiting by the safe spot. I weaved slowly toward him thinking of how I would tell him to stop calling me Becky and what the repercussions would be. I fluttered beside the branch he was perched on unsure of where things would end up.

"Hi Becky," he said proudly. I still didn't like the sound of it no matter who was saying it.

"You know," I started with trepidation; "I really don't like to be called Becky."

"Oh, I'm sorry," he said with surprise. "Shelby said you liked it."

"Shelby? Why would you listen to anything Shelby says?"

"She said you two are close. She said you hang out all the time in the summer."

"I don't even know where she lives." I laughed.

"Oh, wow, I'm really sorry," he said.

I felt genuine remorse in his eem as I fluttered before him. "It's okay," I said.

"Are you going to at least sit with me?"

The feelings of comfort and trust we had developed over the past week returned and, feeling fairly certain I would not be choked, I said, "Sure," as I landed on the branch about a foot to his right.

"What should I call you then?" he asked.

"Rebecca is good," I replied.

"But that's like three syllables."

"It's only one more than Becky."

"But you should have a nickname."

"Why?"

"I don't know," he said, "Nicknames are cool. They are terms of endearment."

"Nicknames are just something other people give you to label you what they want you to be," I began. "Maybe, if they fit really well, they can be okay. Sometime, somewhere, someone will call me a name that will fit really well and it will be cool, but for now, I'm happy with my name."

"Okay, I understand," he said. "How about you give me a chance to find you a nickname anyway?"

"Sure, go for it," I said, "but no derivations of my name like Reba, or Becky or Reb, I really don't like Reb."

We settled into the branches and listened to the wind rustle the leaves on the trees. Rhine stared intently at me for a minute and blurted out, "Slick!"

"What?" I laughed.

"You're fast and kind of slippery…" he explained.

"Kind of slippery?"

"Okay, maybe not slippery," he explained.

"I don't think so."

"Yeah, maybe you're right," he said. "Maybe if I sit closer to you I can get a better feel for your aura."

Rhine slid over beside me until our arms and hips were touching. I was amused by his silly antics as he closed his eyes and took deep breaths. "Nope, still not getting anything. This could be tough. Maybe if I put my arm around you," he said as he reached his right arm between my wings and my back, grasped my right shoulder and pulled me closer. I giggled slightly as he took a couple more deep breaths and said, "Nope, still not getting anything. Maybe if I put my cheek against yours," and he gently pressed his cheek against mine and took another deep breath.

"Still nothing?" I asked.

"Nope, nothing," he replied.

"Well let's see if this helps," I said then placed my hands on both sides of his face, turned it toward mine and pressed my lips against his. I had no idea what I was doing but it didn't matter. It only became an issue when I realized I was kissing a boy and started thinking about the many pointers Kailee and Cora had given me.

Don't press too hard. Keep your lips firm but relaxed. Pretend like you are chewing with your lips. Don't use any tongue. Before I knew it, it was over. I have no idea if I did it right or what "right" really is. All I remember is that I was happy and we gave each other a big hug afterward and that it was special. It was also out of the way. The pressure of my first kiss was gone and, like Kailee said, it was no big deal.

CHAPTER SEVENTEEN

My Dark Side Surfaces

*R*hine and I didn't last much past the first kiss. He started getting real clingy and wanted to be around me all the time and seemed like he felt he had to protect me. All this really cut into my time with Kailee and Cora and time I wanted to just spend by myself. I finally had to tell him that it just wasn't working out as boyfriend and girlfriend but I still wanted to be his friend. He agreed that things weren't as easy as they started out to be and that we should split up. I was glad that he took it so well, or so I thought.

The next day, Rhine and the flying team sat at the same branch with me at lunch but not as closely as before. Only Brent sat in his same perch—across from me a couple branches down. The rest of the kids in the tree watched intently as the team gradually moved away from me and ultimately to their old branch with the Popular kids. This was Shelby's chance.

"Did you know that we are homosexuals?" said Kailee after school.

"What?!" I exclaimed.

"Lesbos to be exact," she added. "That's what they're telling everyone."

"Who?"

"Who do you think?"

"Really? Lesbos?" I chuckled.

"I'm gonna get that witch," said Cora as she approached. "She told everyone we're lesbos. That doesn't even make sense."

"Well I can see where they might believe it about me. I broke up with the only boyfriend I ever had after only two weeks and he was one of the stars on the flying team. We've seen it before."

"But not about us," said Kailee,

"They were going to get to us sooner or later," I said.

"What should we do?" asked Cora.

"It will all blow over if we just leave it alone," I said.

"These stories have a shelf life of about two days; a week at most."

But Shelby and Taylor and Kendra, for whatever reason, seemed to have a bigger grudge against us. Maybe it was because we were their exact opposites. Maybe it was because we didn't fear them like the other kids. Maybe it was because we seemed to be happy regardless of what life threw at us. Whatever it was, they wanted us to pay.

The next week they chose to revisit Kailee's boy exploits from the previous year. They said she was trying to hide her homosexual preferences by dating every boy she could find. While it is not unusual for homosexuals to do just that and sometimes to take it to another extreme and rail against homosexuals and even fight against things like gay rights, Kailee was not one of these fairies and the accusation garnered more laughs than whispers from the school. Having failed at debilitating the more outgoing fairy of our trio, the Evils decided to expand the lie beyond the school and our immediate group.

By the third week the lie had grown to include Cora's dad. They said that he was at a gay camp on the other side of the valley and not really working in the woods. It was, as they had hoped, just plausible enough that the whole school was back on board the lie train. The story put salt in the wound that Cora carried with her every day. But Cora, reluctant to bring her family's troubles into the limelight, let it go in hopes that it would blow over. It didn't.

The final week, the story grew to my mother who they also said was a lesbian. They said she was artificially inseminated because she wanted a child but not a husband and that my father had not died in a leaf painting accident. Had the first part not been so preposterous I would have been more worried about the truth of the second part getting out. But it also stood to reason that the preposterous lie of Mother being homosexual would be assumed correct if the truth of me not knowing who my father was had been discovered. Things were getting dangerous.

"Well, I've had enough," I said to Kailee and Cora after school.

"Finally," shouted Kailee, "What're you gonna do about it?"

"You gonna start a lie about them?" asked Cora.

"Nope, worse," I said confidently.

"What's worse?" asked Kailee.

"We're going to hit them where it hurts," I said.

"Where, in the boobs?" asked Cora.

"I mean it figuratively," I corrected. "What are their most prized possessions?"

"I wouldn't call them possessions but they always brag about their boyfriends," asked Cora.

"They're nothing special," said Kailee. "They think they're all that because they're on the flying team."

"I agree that they are no great prizes," I added, "but, what if we went after them anyway? I mean, what would be worse than losing your boyfriend to a lesbo?"

Kailee and Cora looked at each other and smiled.

"The winter social is coming up. Wouldn't it be ripe if

their boyfriends were our dates?"

"How do we do that?" asked Cora. "I mean Shelby is so slutty. She always wears her tops so at least one bra strap is showing…"

"… and she's always hanging all over Dre," added Kailee. "Who knows how far she's gone with him?"

"We'll have to take some chances," I said. "We'll have to change our clothes and the way we carry ourselves. But it can be done."

"How do you know?" asked Cora.

"Have you ever watched her mom?" asked Kailee rhetorically.

"Trust me, I learned from the best," I answered.

CHAPTER EIGHTEEN

Taking on the Evils

We had the weekend to get our act together. We only had a month before the Winter Social. Kailee really didn't need any tips; she just needed permission to turn it all loose. Cora was already graceful and articulate, now we needed to turn her into a flirt, or even better, a tease. Since we had no classes together, we had to work each target alone which meant Cora needed to be ready for almost any situation. We would start with our clothes.

Kailee and Cora were already wearing "foothill" cup size bras. We just left a couple more buttons undone on their tops so the "girls" weren't hidden so much. The good thing about buttoned tops was that we could keep the image of sweet and innocent at home and, with a few minor adjustments like untucking the shirt and tying the shirttails around our waist, we had the trampy look we were going for at school. Shredded pant legs were allowed in school but holes had to be covered. The good kids simply wore pants without holes. Our tramp look used vines tied around our legs to cover our indiscretions. Even better was wearing a skirt because only a real tease would wear a skirt to school in the winter. Monday came and we were ready.

Heads turned as we bounced into the school. Bouncing when you are flying is kind of like strutting to humans; and we had the bounce working! The boys were drooling and the girls were scowling. We accompanied the bounce with big smiles and the occasional wink to the boys and quick smiles and a fake, "Hi," with a quaint wave to the girls. We bounced our way into the building and straight to the bathroom where we slammed the door and blocked it.

"Yes!" shouted Kailee as she and Cora slapped a hi-five.

"O-M-G!" said Cora, "did you just see that?"

"Okay, okay, let's not lose sight of our mission," I said calmly. "They'll all get over the shock of today. We have to keep this up for a month."

"Right," said Cora, still beaming from the entrance.

"And you've got to know that the Evils will come up with something else to say about us," added Kailee.

"It could get pretty messy," I said.

"They made it messy when they lied about my dad," said Cora.

"Okay, this first week we see who falls for who. To maximize our chances of success, we will go after the boy that goes for us regardless of whose boyfriend it is. Also, absolutely no going after anyone outside the target area. Any boy that didn't ask you out before because they thought you were a lesbo doesn't deserve you now. Keep your eye on the prize. Dre, Spike and Clave, that's it."

"Right," agreed Kailee.

"Right," said Cora nodding her head.

"Okay, girls, time to go to work," I said and opened the door to our trampy new world.

I didn't realize how much work would be involved in pulling this off. I had to be "on" all the time and use whatever tricks I had available whenever the opportunity presented itself. One especially teasing thing I remember Mother doing on occasion was not crossing her rudder wings when she bent over to get a drink of water from a stream or fountain. Not crossing your rudder wings always implied that others might see the small growth at the end of your spine that was called a tail. Uncrossed rudder wings also implied that you were ready to mate. Brent caught me doing this between second and third period.

"What'cha doin'?" he said abruptly as he flew with me toward my next class.

"Hi Brent," I replied.

"No, what are you doing?" he clarified. "This is not you."

"Really?" I answered. "Maybe it is. Maybe I got tired of the old me."

"What was wrong with the old you?"

"The old me was boring. I need some excitement."

"Does this mean you're giving up on Touch-and-Go too?"

"Maybe."

"Maybe?"

"It's winter. No one plays in the winter," I said while flashing a smile to another boy we passed.

"No one says you can't play Touch-and-Go in the winter. You want to play today?"

"Not today. I have things to do."

"Like what? Homework?"

"Yeah, homework."

"How about after that?"

"I have a lot of homework."

Brent shook his head, "I don't know what's going on here but I don't like it. You'd better be careful or you may stay this way."

It sounded like a warning Mother would say; "Be careful or your face might stay that way." The difference was Brent was right. I just didn't know it at the time.

For the next three weeks Kailee, Cora and I worked the plan to perfection. We had almost every boy in the school eating out of the palms of our hands. The Evils started a number of rumors about us that no one believed because we just laughed at them and we were, after all, the hottest girls in the school. With one week to go, the targets identified themselves. Clave, Kendra's boyfriend, had taken a special liking to Kailee. Spike, Taylor's boyfriend, was paying special attention to Cora. I got Dre and the chance to get what everybody in the school wanted; revenge against Shelby.

The goal was to get each of these boys to dump their girlfriends and ask us to the Winter Social. It had to happen soon because even these guys aren't mean enough to dump their girlfriends the day before the dance. It was time to ramp up the charm.

Mother was an expert at hooking the fish and reeling him into her net. The secret is to know when to pull on the line and when to let the fish run a little. First we had to get them to bite. That was done by simply giving them some attention. In a room or hallway filled with boys, all looking at you, you just bounce over to your target and ask flirtatiously if he might lend you a pencil, or let you lean on him while you scratch your foot, or if he would "be so kind as to loosen the strap on my frontpack just a smidge." That usually garners a few "oohs" from the other boys to whom you just smile.

The reeling in requires a little more time commit- ment and the ability to act dumb if you aren't a truly dumb person. It is said that boys don't like smart girls. I haven't found this to be completely true. I think there are plenty of males who like smart women but there isn't a man or boy who doesn't want to feel needed. That is why women ask for help. For this mission, we asked for help with homework. Math is one of those subjects in which boys like to think they are superior. Ideally, the male target is in your class and you can simply wander up to him after a seemingly troubling chapter and say, "I really don't get any of this. Is there a chance you might have some time after school to tutor me a little?" If the target happens to be too dumb to help with homework, you simply play to their physical strengths and ask for help lifting or moving something at home. Either way, the goal is to be alone with the target for an extended period of time.

The capture or netting is when he asks you out. This is difficult if the target is already going out with someone else—unless he is a jerk who just jumps from girl to girl on a whim, in which case, who wants him?

Clave and Dre definitely fell into this category but Spike didn't seem like the type. But we had something that would entice them to pull the trigger. We had the Evil's lie. You see, most boys are not afraid of a challenge, if the prize is big enough. We were the prize and a pretty big one after our work the last three weeks. The challenge; turning a "lesbo" straight. Now Kailee, Cora and I knew that the whole lesbian thing was a joke but the boys didn't. The Evils took one last run at us by telling everyone we were only dressing and acting this way to hide our homosexuality. That only helped us. Once we had Dre, Spike and Clave alone, we threw down the fully scripted challenge.

"So," said Kailee as she slid over and bumped her shoulder into Clave in the library, "you want to take me to the Winter Social?"

"But, don't you like girls?" questioned Clave.

"To be honest, I'm a little confused about the whole lesbo thing," said Cora as she twirled her finger in her hair across the table from Spike in the cafeteria.

"How is someone confused about their sexuality?" asked Spike.

I scooted in close to Dre at his family's kitchen table, put the tip of my index finger under his chin, slowly spun his face toward mine and whispered, "You know, you could be the one to change me." Each one of us closed with this dramatic line and we all had dates for the dance the next week.

We arrived at school the next morning to find Shelby, Kendra and Taylor in front of the tree and the rest of the eighth grade lining our approach. We did our usual bounce through the gauntlet to maintain the image we had set the past four weeks and stopped face-to-face with our rivals.

"Hello, ladies; and I use the term loosely," I said.

"Our boyfriends say they have different dates for the dance this weekend," said Shelby.

"What a coincidence," said Kailee, "we have new dates for the dance this weekend."

"I should rip your wings off," said Kendra.

"Yeah, you should," countered Cora, "but lies and deceit are more your style, aren't they? You should have left our families alone."

"I think everyone is pretty tired of your act," I said.

"You're just a bunch of whores," was Shelby's retort.

I just laughed. "That's it? Whores?" I just shook my head "I expected something more creative from the three of you." We pushed our way passed the three angry girls and headed toward the school. "This was very disappointing," I added.

"This isn't over," shouted Shelby.

"Girl, you are going to have to go all-in to win this one," I smirked. The school bird chirped and an entire school population followed us in.

The week was intense. I kept looking over my shoulder for some type of physical attack from the Evils or one of their henchmen all the while keeping my flirtatious facade in tact. I was back to eating lunch alone with my back to the trunk. Dre had a different lunch period and the rest of the school was waiting for some type of retaliation, too. Brent didn't want to be around the new me. I didn't want to be around the new me either.

Kailee, Cora and I went dress shopping and spent most of the time trying to convince ourselves of how wonderful our dates were. None of us felt compelled to get the best gown in the shop. The only dresses left on the sale branches were Summery, off-the-shoulder styles that were totally inappropriate for the event. We each bought one proclaiming we would make the event even more festive. Mine was dark blue with large, white lilies.

Fortunately the charade was almost over. The dance was in two days. Kailee, Cora and I could thank our dates for a nice evening and go back to being ourselves having stuck Shelby, Taylor and Kendra with substitutes or no dates at all for the biggest dance of the year. But plans change.

"Rebecca!" hollered Kailee over the crowd in the hall. School was over for the day and everyone was gathering for an especially frigid fly home. The wind howled as a cold front dipped down from Canada. Fortunately there would be no snow but it still didn't make flying any easier. "Rebecca!" Kailee called again and again until she finally caught up to me. "Come here," she said as she dragged me into the bathroom and closed the door. "Dre is going to the dance with

114

Shelby," she said. First I was surprised and then a little angry and then relieved. "Shelby is going to mate with him," she continued.

"What?!" I exclaimed.

"Everyone's talking about it."

"What about Taylor and Kendra?" I asked. "Are they being stupid too?"

"I haven't heard anything about them," said Kailee. "I don't think they're that desperate."

"Wow. That girl has got some real issues," I said as I paced around the bathroom thinking.

"What are you going to do?" asked Kailee.

"I have to find her and stop her," I determined.

"You're not going to offer to mate with Dre, are you?" Kailee asked sternly.

"NO! Are you kidding?! I don't care about Dre," I exclaimed.

"Sorry, gee," she replied.

"I can't let Shelby do this to herself," I said. "Let me out. I need to try and catch her before she leaves."

I darted out the door and into a much less congested hallway. I rushed toward the exit that I knew Shelby left from each day and stopped at the door that opened to the cold and windy day. On days like this, it is better to travel in groups—the extra bodies help keep each other warm and cut through the wind. I saw Taylor and Kendra waiting outside with

Dre, but no Shelby. I turned around to see her coming my way. She stopped in the hallway when she saw me.

"I told you it wasn't over," she smirked.

"You're not really going to do it, are you?" I started. "You're just telling him that so he'll go to the dance with you, right?"

"Do what?" she said coyly.

"Mate with him," I said. "Everyone is talking about it."

"If everyone's talking about it then it must be true," she confirmed smugly.

"Don't do it," I begged.

"You're just mad because I got my boyfriend back," she argued.

"Take him, I don't really care," I said. "Go to the dance. Have a great time. Just don't mate with him. You're too young. He's too young. We're all too young to take those kinds of chances." Kailee and Cora appeared in the hall behind Shelby. "Don't you think we should wait until we're ready to have kids of our own?" I continued. "You know that's why we mate, don't you? To make babies?"

"I'm not stupid," she said.

"Please, don't do it," I pleaded. For a moment, the impenetrable emotional walls that had forever insulated Shelby began to lower and I began to feel the pain in her eem. But the walls shot back up when she heard the flutter of wings behind her and looked back to see Kailee and Cora.

"I've got this under control," she said coldly then stormed past me and out into the cold. A harsh wind slammed the door closed on the only chance I had to truly connect with her. I stood in the doorway feeling sympathy for the girl I once despised.

"What are you going to do about the dance," asked Kailee.

"Looks like I'm going to have to find somewhere else to go in a semi-formal summer dress," I replied.

"Are you going to be all right?" asked Cora.

"It's just a dance," I said with a sigh. "You ready to go home? It looks nasty out there."

"I'll take the lead," said Cora. "I'm feeling strong today."

"I'll take the back," said Kailee. "Looks like you could use a little lift," she said to me. We closed up our coats a little tighter, strapped on our frontpacks a little firmer and walked out to see Dre give a timid-looking Shelby a quick kiss before they, Taylor and Kendra flew off in a diamond formation.

"She already did it, didn't she?" said Cora.

"I think so," I said.

"Should we tell everyone?" asked Kailee.

"I've got a feeling her friends have already done that," I said.

CHAPTER NINETEEN

One Last Charade

riday night came and I didn't have a date. The rumor of Shelby mating with Dre the night of the dance was already the talk of school. Some assumed it had already happened while others professed to know where and when the event would actually take place. The only good thing about it was that no one was talking about me anymore. I was plenty happy with the anonymity. Of course I wasn't completely ignored since I no longer had a date to the dance and decided I didn't need to keep up the facade I had created to steal Dre away from Shelby in the first place. At least people still respected me which was more than could be said for "Shelby the slut" as she was soon labeled. Granted, every girl in middle school was referred to as a slut by someone at some time but Shelby was self proclaimed and I'm still not sure if she was proud of it at the time. But she and Dre were no longer my problem. My problem was finding something to do in my new dress that Friday night other than go to the dance.

You see, Mother didn't know that I had lost my date and I didn't think she needed to know. She also didn't know about our scheme to steal our dates for the dance and I didn't think she needed to know about that either. Her life was complicated enough and besides, she wouldn't understand. So Friday arrived and Mother was waiting at home to help me get ready. She loved dressing me up. It gave us a chance to talk about boys and school and the many things we no longer seemed to have time for. But I had concocted other plans which I made known as I fluttered toward the door with my dress still on a hanger and a bag with my brushes in my arms.

"Where are you going?" Mother asked a little shocked.

"Cora and I are meeting at Kailee's house to get dressed and everything," I answered.

"Oh," she said disheartened, "I thought I would be helping you get ready."

"Oh, sorry," I said, "we planned this when we were shopping. I thought I told you about it."

"You didn't mention it," she said.

"Really? I'm pretty sure I told you," I lied.

"I'm pretty sure you didn't," she calmly replied. "I left work early to make dinner and to be here to help you."

"I'm sorry, I thought you had someone coming over tonight," I said. This was a low blow because Mother seldom had anyone over to the house and she typically only cooked for male friends who were helping her with a project.

"No, not tonight," she said while maintaining her calm.

Had my eem with her not faded so much over the past years, she most likely would have known I was lying. Continuing the lie was getting harder and harder. After all, I wasn't really going to Kailee's. I just needed a way to get out of the house with the dress. Seeing the disappointment on her face was heartbreaking.

"It smells good," I said. "I can stay and have dinner and go over to Kailee's a little later."

"That would be nice," said Mother.

I hung the dress on an exposed branch in the ceiling and fluttered into the kitchen where Mother had set two bowls with spinach leaves, raisins and walnuts all covered in plum juice. Hot water on the heating element boiled pasta and somehow she had procured some butter to melt on it. Usually human things, like pasta and butter, had to be purchased from a mischief fairy who took it from a human house. Both were considered delicacies. Pasta with butter was one of my favorite foods. Finally, beside my bowl and plate, lay a beautiful white lily corsage. I crouched on the perch and gently picked up the flower.

"I thought it would go nicely with your dress," she said.

"It's very nice," I said. "How did you get the butter?"

"Ingrid got it for me last night," she said as she poured the water from the pot. "It goes bad if you don't use it right away."

"I can't believe you did all of this. Where did you find fresh fruit and vegetables in the winter?"

"I went to a human grocery store late last night. I find that around three o'clock is a good time. The doors they have are never closed and the places seem virtually empty. I just flew in, grabbed what I needed and flew out."

"They didn't see you?"

"I don't think so," she said as she spooned out the noodles and placed slices of butter on the small piles. "Besides, what are they going to say? Most of them don't believe in fairies. But that's not important now. You have to go soon and I don't know anything about your date."

I did my best to avoid eye contact and began to pick at my food.

"He's not that great. Just another boy," I said.

"What's his name?"

"Dre."

"Dre?" she wondered.

"Yeah, Dre," I replied as I stuffed spinach into my mouth.

"I thought he was Shelby's boyfriend?"

"He dumped her about a week ago."

"Oh, I guess I hadn't heard that," she said. "And you swooped in and gathered him up? That's unlike you."

"He asked me," I said. "I didn't have a date so I said yes. It's really no big deal."

"Oh."

"I mean, look at the dress I bought," I added. "It was on sale. We're just friends."

"Oh," she said. "So, does he know that you aren't really that interested in him?"

"I'm certain," I answered confidently. It was a relief to tell the truth.

"That's too bad," she said. "I remember my eighth grade winter dance. Keep in mind, winter in Louisiana is nothing compared to here. But we still wore darker colors and decorated the hall with an igloo. I think winter is the most romantic because the sun goes down earlier and the stars are especially bright since the humidity is lower. I went with Talon. He was from a good family and spoke well. He was gentle and graceful and he told me I was beautiful. We stayed out late and watched the bats and owls hunt by the light of a full moon."

"Did you kiss him?" I asked.

"Rebecca, my dear, have I taught you nothing," she said. "A lady never kisses a man. But I did let him kiss

122

me." She and I shared a playful smile. "You had better eat up. I'm sure Kailee is expecting you before dusk."

"You're right," I said uncomfortably. "Thank you for making dinner." I slowly rose from the perch and fluttered toward the door. I no longer felt like going through with the charade but had just talked myself deeper into the story and felt I needed to finish it. I draped the dress over my arm, gathered my make-up bag and turned toward my mom. "Don't wait up for me," I smiled.

"I will go to bed if I get too tired," she smiled. "Have fun," she said as I closed the door behind me.

CHAPTER TWENTY

A Dark and Stormy Night

*T*he reflection in a small pond of a blue dress with white lilies was the last thing I saw before I darted toward the full moon in a cloudy night sky. I thought tonight I might try to actually touch the moon since I had nothing else to do for the next three or four or five hours. I would be sure to be back in time to put on my dress and make-up before going home. I might not have to do that either if I stayed out late enough. But five hours is a long time to waste. First I went to the dance to see what accessories Kailee and Cora had chosen and to get a glimpse of the decorations so I could keep that part of the story straight when Mother asked.

I stared into the windows of the beautiful but fairyless building. There were silver streamers and paper snowflakes hung from the ceiling and penguins on an iceberg. There was a big furry abominable snow fairy perched in one corner above the beverage bar that was made of real ice. Ice and Snow Fairies that chaperoned the dance kept things from melting and ultimately provided real snow for the slow dances and the first dance of the King and Queen who were elected by the eighth grade students. I was sure Brent and Breezy would win again. The whole thing looked like fun and I suddenly wished I was still going. I briefly considered going alone but, after blowing a whole month stealing someone's boyfriend just to get dumped the day before the dance, that wasn't going to happen. I hid in the trees and watched everyone else flutter toward the school. Most of the girls wore some version of winter fairy attire except Kailee and Cora who maintained the summery, flowery theme of our original plan. They eventually arrived with Clave and Spike and looked like they were having fun.

Cora told me how Spike made her laugh and actually listened when she talked and shared some of the same opinions. She found herself slipping out of the dumb girl character we had created and realized that he liked her better as a smart person. The makeup and clothing styles we were pushing to the limits brought her out of her shell though, and she found a happy medium between her 'before' and 'after' looks, with no negative affects on the relationship.

Kailee didn't have to reach too far to play her seductress role. What Clave saw was what Clave got and he was more than happy to oblige Kailee's every need and desire, even if the relationship was temporary. Everything with Kailee was temporary in eighth grade. I watched the four smiling and laughing partiers flutter hand-in-hand into the gym.

Thinking I was sufficiently armed with the necessary data to convincingly lie my way through mother's eventual interrogation, I gradually backed out of the tree stopping briefly to watch Shelby and Dre pass below. She clung to Dre's arm like a baby monkey holds onto its mother. Her large smile and dramatic arm motions were even more ostentatious than before. Dre strutted along grinning to the guys touching knuckles in lieu of handshakes. I assumed Shelby had fulfilled her promise. I felt sad that she felt the need to mate with someone in order for him to like her. I continued my slow retreat until I was out of earshot then darted toward the sky.

The winds above the trees were turbulent. It was as if they knew what I was up to and were not going to let anything about this night be easy. No matter which direction I turned, I was flying into the wind. I stiffened my body into the most aerodynamic position I knew and beat my wings with quick, short strokes to push me forward. This did little more than make me tired. I opted instead to drop below the tops of the trees and weave through the swaying, leafless branches. It was less physically draining but a greater mental challenge as my path changed with every gust of wind. The trees swayed so much that I found myself stepping from branch to branch. I may as well have been a human given the lack of opportunities I had to use my wings.

All I wanted to do was go to the outer edge of the colony, perch on a branch and have a few moments of peace looking at the moon and the few bright stars that might shine through the clouds. But after two hours of work I had only gotten half way to my destination. And then the air became heavy with the musty smell that always precedes rain and I thought of my dress hanging on the tree beside the creek. I threw caution to the violent winds and shot down toward the ground. I would have to fly the entire way under the lower branches to save time. The cats and foxes and coyotes were smarter than to be out in a rain storm in the winter anyway.

Rain drops slapped the naked sticks and twigs as the storm chased me to my dress. If I was lucky, I would have a minute or two to slip it on before the rain soaked it against my body—clothes are so much easier to put on when they are dry. But when I arrived, all I saw was the empty hanger with my make-up bag swinging from the branch. I could hear the rain drops approaching over my panting. Where was my dress?! Why would someone take my dress?

I knew that nobody had taken my dress, that was stupid. Maybe the wind blew it onto another branch. So on a dark stormy night, I began climbing through bare branches looking for a dark blue dress with white lilies. I ran scenarios through my head of how I would explain the damage to mother that could be anything from small tears on the trim to totally ravaged. The explanations ranged from an impromptu Touch-and-Go game to jealous girls at school ripping my clothes off. I didn't expect her to totally buy into the last one but it was all I had. The rain drops fell with a vengeance and there was nowhere safe to hide. Defeated, I sat down beside the trunk of the tree, closed my eyes, took a deep breath and listened. I always liked to listen to the rain as it hit the roof of the house and the leaves and the pond and the ground. Those sounds were familiar and safe and for a few minutes I felt peaceful.

But the sounds were inconsistent and soon I discerned the unusual sound of rain drops thudding onto my dress that lay in the pond below. I shook loose the water that had gathered on my wings, swooped down and scooped the gown from the water. Holding it out in front of me, I examined both sides the best I could for rips and tears and stains which was no easy task with the darkness and wind and rain. Most importantly I had to get it on and, given the somewhat tight nature of the design, it wasn't easy. Fortunately, it was sleeveless. The shawl was gone and I didn't have time for make-up if I wanted to make it home before my wings waterlogged. I shook myself off again and, leaving everything else behind, headed for home.

CHAPTER TWENTY-ONE

The Turning Point

The air quickly turned icy (as it can do in Colorado) and the moisture that fell from the sky became a mixture of rain and snow. I was forced to stop after every couple of trees to shake off my wings. This paired with fighting the wind all night had me exhausted by the time I reached the edge of the colony which, from a distance, looked like a Christmas tree. Almost every house had candles lit. Most of the families had a child at the Winter Dance and I was sure the rain had many parents concerned for the safety of their teenagers. I shook the rain and snow from my wings one more time and darted toward my porch hoping Mother was already asleep. A light glowed from inside our home, too. I landed on the branch beside the porch and tried to gather myself physically and mentally. Mostly I just wanted to put the whole night behind me and go to bed. I opened the door and stepped into the house to see Mother sitting on the rocking perch rolling the stem of the lily I had left behind between her fingers. Her eyes focused on the twirling flower at the end of the stem.

"Hi," I said casually, "You're still up."

There was a brief pause before she replied with a simple, "Yes."

"It's starting to snow so I came home early," I added.

"That sounds like a smart thing to do," she remarked coolly.

"My dress got soaked and I may have snagged it on some branches along the way. The wind is really blowing."

"Did Dre leave early too?"

"No. He stayed with his friends. Everyone else was too scared to fly in the rain."

"I'm kind of surprised that they let you leave," she said. "How was it?"

"What, the dance?"

"Wherever you were tonight."

"It was okay," I began. "The decorations were nice. They had a bar made of real ice and an Abominable Snow Fairy hanging over it. They had those paper snowflakes hanging from the ceiling and a fake iceberg with penguins. The music was the usual dance stuff…"

Mother quietly shook her head with disgust and simply said, "Wow." Then she stepped from the perch and, still not able to bring herself to look at me, headed toward the stairs. "I deserve better than this," she muttered on her way past me. Then she said it again as she shook her head at the base of the stairs. "I really do deserve better than this."

"What?" I asked having honestly not heard the comment.

Then she looked at me and articulated through clenched teeth, "I deserve better than this!"

"What are you talking about?!" I replied pretending I didn't know the reason for the statement.

"Oh don't play dumb with me. You know exactly what I'm talking about!" she argued as the volume rose.

"No, I don't," I yelled back. "Is it that I forgot to take the flower?"

"Really?" she asked sarcastically.

"I'm sorry, okay. I'm sorry I forgot to take the stupid flower."

"You know what, just go on. Be that way. I've had enough of your lies for one day. I deserve better than this." She turned up the stairs toward her room.

"Maybe you don't deserve better than this," I shouted. She stopped in her tracks. "Look at my role model," I continued. "The acorn doesn't fall far from the tree." She moved slowly down the stairs as I continued my ill-fated rant. "Who are you to preach about right and wrong? Look at how you treat people; especially men. You lead them on and trick them into doing things for you then toss them away when they no longer have anything you need. Did you think I wouldn't figure out how you got the bedroom done? You're nothing better than a slut and a whore."

A look of anger took over Mother's face as she dropped the flower and flew toward me with her right arm and empty hand out to her side. When she reached me her arm spun around and her hand landed flush against my cheek with a loud slap. There was a rush of emotion that included anger and astonishment quickly followed by sadness and revenge. The intensity of every-thing collapsing on me at once was too much. The only thing I could do was cry.

"How dare you talk to me like that you selfish little...? I can't believe you think you can treat me like some stupid kid you abuse at school because you're popular. You lie to my face and demean me behind my back and for what; to improve your status with your friends? I deserve better than that. I deserve much bet-ter than that!"

She tried to calm herself but the frustration of years of mental abuse, combined with the anger with herself for hitting me, and the knowledge that an apology from her at this point would be counter-productive (because I really deserved what I had gotten) kept her from being able to settle her nerves. She paced angrily looking for the right thing to say while fighting the urge to comfort me ultimately realizing that the only thing that would give her any peace was to not see me for awhile.

All of her emotions streamed directly to me through her eem and I felt all of her pain as if it was my own just as she had felt my frustration moments earlier. "Get out," she said remorsefully, "your friends are obviously more important to you than me. Why don't you just go over there?"

"But it's raining and snowing outside," I cried.

"You seemed to find your way home in the same weather from wherever you were tonight. Why don't you just fly fast like you do in Touch-and-Go?" she answered. "I would tell you to wear a coat but you wouldn't listen to me anyway."

"Kailee and Cora aren't home; they're at the dance," I cried.

"I don't care where you go, you don't get to be in my home," she said sternly. I still sat crying in the perch.

"Go on!" she shouted, "I don't want you here!"

I slowly stood and dragged myself toward the door. "How long do I have to be gone?" I asked.

"I don't know," she said. "Long enough for me to forgive you. Long enough for me to forgive myself." I slipped on my jacket and opened the door to leave. "By the way, you were voted queen of the dance," she interrupted. "Brent came by in his crown looking for you."

To be honest, I don't remember how I felt when she told me that. I was focused on finding a place to spend a few hours or possibly the rest of my life. I'm sure Kailee's or Cora's parents would have taken me in for the night but they would have wanted to know why I wasn't home and I didn't feel like explaining the past month's events to people when I didn't understand them myself. I flew to the most comfortable place I knew, the safe spot on the old Cottonwood tree, and huddled under my jacket while my mind raced.

What had I done? How could I have let it go this far? What was wrong with me? I had called my mother a name I hadn't used to describe my worst enemy. Worst of all, she was right; I was guilty of doing everything she accused me of.

I was scared and sad and worried that my only parent didn't love me any more. She actually slapped me in the face. When I was younger, she would, on rare occasions, give me a swat on the butt when I did something that was disrespectful. Those times were scary enough but to be hit in the face was far and beyond what I could comprehend. And the pain and frustration I felt in her eem was something I didn't expect. I always thought that parents did what they wanted and were impervious to emotional pain. After all, they were the boss and we children had to do whatever we were told.

But I hadn't done what I was told or even what I knew to be right for the past month. I wore clothing that I could make look sleazy when I went to school; I played dumb and stopped doing my homework; I found myself disagreeing with almost everything Mother suggested simply for the sake of disagreeing. I had become Becky—everything I abhorred. And what was worse, I had stayed Becky—just as Brent had warned. I needed to go back to being Rebecca.

My mind had been so preoccupied that I hadn't noticed that the wind had stopped blowing and the rain had turned to a light snow. Snowflakes now floated all around me and the moonlight that forced itself through the clouds bounced off the new white blanket on the ground. Seeing my breath in the air before me after a deep sigh reminded me that I was cold. I needed to get inside. I just didn't know where. I half expected to hear the familiar "what'cha doin'" from Brent but instead heard something better.

"Rebecca," called Mother as she glided toward the safe spot.

"Mom?" I called back.

"If you prefer, 'mom' is fine," she said as she wrapped her arms around me and held me tight.

"I'm sorry," I cried.

"Me too," she said.

We held each other for a few more seconds before

135

she said, "We need to get inside before these tears freeze." We held each other's hand as we flew at a comfortable pace toward home.

"How did you know where I was?" I asked.

"Honestly, Rebecca," she said, "Do you think I don't know my own daughter?"

CHAPTER TWENTY-TWO

The Big Fish

*H*igh school was nothing compared to middle school. There were still cliques and some gossip but everyone seemed to "find themselves" and an appropriate set of peers with whom to associate. Shelby moved to a new colony and Kendra and Taylor stopped looking for people to pick on. I don't know if the proverbial snake was killed when its head was cut off by Shelby moving or if Kendra and Taylor simply became more comfortable with who they were as they got older. It was also rumored that Shelby had a new baby. Dre, however, was still with us.

Cora drifted away as she focused on more technical things like science and math. I did have her in one math class in tenth grade but I focused more on creative endeavors; things like leaf painting and tree and bush molding. Tree and bush molding involves determining the best places for branches to grow so as to create stronger trees and plants and better environments for the animals that will utilize them. The best Molding Fairies know everything about each tree and bush they work with and exactly how to wand them so the new branches will be strong and the trunks will not be injured. I could understand how Mother would want to work in this field and her desire to develop new plants and trees as a botanist.

The biggest change for me came when I made the Touch-and-Go team my first year. It wasn't a big surprise to anyone who knew me. Brent and Rhine were kind of glad to not have to play against me anymore. But even Touch-and-Go began to lose its appeal. I later learned that the game was created by the elders as a way to find the future Tooth and Mischief fairies. Both needed to be quick, agile and somewhat fearless since they were constantly in the presence of humans and couldn't afford to be caught.

At the start of my last year, a new player made the team. His name was Lake and he was one of the rare nice and rich guys in the colony. His family owned the large Ash tree their home was in and had water rights from the stream. Owning a tree was a big deal because it meant that you could make money by renting out homes on the lower branches to other fairies. The water rights weren't a big deal unless there was a drought and we couldn't capture rain water. Lake moved here from

Texas where he said the air was more humid and flying was harder because his wings were always heavy with moisture. He could see why we were known for being so fast and was excited when he made the team. He was genuine and smart and polite; everything I wanted in a man. And he liked me, too.

We would spend days studying and laughing and flying to the edge of the colony where we would sit on the upper branches of our favorite Maple tree and hold hands and even kiss on occasion. On bad days we would just hold each other. My bad days usually were caused by school or Mother. His bad days were typically the result of something to do with his parents. But his parents seemed to like me. They were impressed at how proper I was and especially noted how well I walked.

Lake told me stories of his life in the south; the heat and the storms and how his parents, who both worked in the Gulf of Mexico, were no longer needed after the great oil spill in twenty-ten. The family grew tired of the dramatic temperature changes and the natural and unnatural disasters that continually affected their colony. Colorado held the best opportunities for nature-based careers and his father really liked mountains.

Everything was going well, I thought. There were snickers amongst the kids in school and Kailee told me to be careful but I didn't see anything from Lake that would cause alarm. But rumors that his parents would not let our relationship go past that year began to surface. Lake just brushed off the stories when I asked about them saying only that his parents didn't run his life. But the stories became more prevalent and Lake became more defiant towards his parents and then more withdrawn around me. It all started to make sense during our last match of Touch-and-Go before graduation.

I think we were battling the team from Columbine. It's not important who it was really, but I remember that it was a close match and Lake's parents were there. They didn't typically come to our matches. I assumed they were there because it was our last. Lake, Brent and I were still in play and the other squad had only two flyers left; one girl and one boy. Lake and I were running a bait-and-tag play with the girl leaving Brent free to catch the boy.

Bait-and-tag plays require one flyer to entice a player to chase them while leading the chaser toward his or her teammate who would touch the chaser and beat the opponent to the safe spot. Lake and I were the best at this. I was the bait because I was very good at slaloming and could always out-fly the other player if I happened to get touched. Plus I was a girl which made the boys think I was an easy target. Lake usually had no problem being the tagger to whom I would lead the other player. It was a pretty easy position to play because the chaser would usually be tired when they were tagged by him. Still fresh from hovering casually in a corner, Lake would easily outrace the opponent to the safe spot. The play accounted for about thirty percent of Lake's tags for the season.

I had done my job and coaxed the girl to come after me. She was very good (as girls must be to make it in a boys' world) and was hard to shake. She was a little bigger than me but not as agile. I was careful to stay just far enough ahead to not be touched but close enough to give the impression she might catch me. I wove through the higher branches and glanced over my shoulder to confirm that Lake was in place. But he wasn't in place.

He was supposed to be in the lower east corner behind the Aspen trees and then was to rise up above the tops of the small cluster as I drew her down to the lower branches giving him the upper angle for the tag. Where was he? I gave my wings a strong flap to get some extra distance from my pursuer as I did another lap around the field. I didn't see him anywhere and I was getting tired. Had we not decided on this play, I would have approached the girl opponent differently and probably just chased her down from above, tagged her, and sprinted to the safe spot. But I was too tired to change my approach. If Lake wasn't in his spot the next time around, I was going to be out of the game and the one player advantage would go to the other side.

My chaser drew closer and took the position above me making it nearly impossible for me to tag her as she approached. Just like when I was four, I squeezed every bit of energy from my body as I turned toward the Aspen trees and dove toward the lower branches one last time. She pushed her wings as hard as she could and came down after me. The buzzing sound of fairy wings flapping grew exponentially louder a split second before she and I heard Brent yell "touch" as he touched her on the head and darted toward the safe spot. She was too tired to even chase him.

We found Lake chasing the boy from the other team on the other side of the field. Brent dove in front of both of them giving Lake a clear shot for the touch. Once touched, the last competitor gave up.

"Where were you?" I interrogated Lake as the team gathered at the safe spot for a brief celebration.

"I had a shot at the other guy," he said.

"You could have let me know," I said. "I made three trips around the field looking for you. If Brent hadn't dived in at the last second I probably would have been caught."

"Sorry," he said defensively. He looked nervously back to where his parents were perched in the trees. I

142

tried to make eye contact and connect with his eem but he wouldn't allow it to happen.

"Are you alright?" I asked. "You've been different these last few days."

"I guess I'm just nervous about graduation," he answered.

I should have known what was coming but I was too naïve or dumb or even maybe in love to believe the rumors. His parents were leery about my interest in Lake. They had continually warned him of girls who would date him because he was wealthy and Mother's self-imposed limit of three dresses did little to assuage their fears.

But Lake loved me. He said so. He had defied his parents by continuing to date me and hadn't even looked at another girl the whole year. Graduation was in a couple days and we were going to the ball that night. Mother helped me buy a beautiful gown to match his tunic. He would pick me up at dusk, as is the tradition, and we would dance and sing and celebrate our new lives with the new wings we would all receive at the ceremony earlier that day. At the end of the evening, as sometimes happens, he might even ask me to be tethered to him which is like being married for humans. But it was all just wishful thinking.

CHAPTER TWENTY-THREE

Still Not Caught

The stars glowed brightly in the sky and the air was warm and dry. The moonlight bounced off my new Tooth Fairy wings which were sleek and sparkly. Brent was also a tooth fairy. Of course the whole graduation ceremony was delayed when Aynil got his Traveler wings but I'll let him tell that story. Tooth fairy wasn't my first choice but I wasn't surprised to get it since they anticipated a shortage due to retirement and I was one of the best flyers in the class.

Music from the dance could be heard in the distance as Mother and I waited inside for Lake to arrive. Mother brushed my long hair one hundred times and helped me pull it back into a ponytail. I really do miss having my hair brushed. I sat on the perch in the front room anxiously waiting for the evening to begin. Mother, dressed to go on her first date in years with Gaylen, quickly cleaned the kitchen as the sun ducked behind the mountains. It was dusk and the front porch candles that would greet the arriving young men magically lit at the same time.

I heard the cheers and calls from the neighboring houses as the young women greeted their dates. With each cry and cheer I became more anxious, ready to feel that same excitement for myself. But the excitement outside subsided almost as quickly as it started; just like it had every year before when I listened and dreamed of what this night might hold for me. In the distance the faint music was now accompanied by laughter and chatter. The party had started without me.

"He must've had a problem," said Mother.

Then came a slow deliberate knock. I rushed to the door, gathered myself, and opened it gracefully using my "bashfully look at the ground and slowly raise my smiling face toward the handsome prince" look only to see Gaylen standing before me.

"You look beautiful," said Gaylen. He looked embarrassed as he handed me a letter and said, "I found this on the branch."

I stepped aside to let him enter as Mother walked in from the kitchen. "What does it say, honey?" she asked.

"I'm sorry," I read. "It's from Lake." I dropped to my knees and stared at the note for a second or a minute or who knows how long. It wasn't until Mother kneeled beside me and wrapped her arm around my back that I started crying.

"What kind of spineless jerk leaves a letter on a tree?" said Gaylen.

"I'm sorry Gaylen, but can we postpone our date?" asked Mother. "I think I'm needed here tonight."

"I understand," he said.

"I'll find you tomorrow if that's okay," said Mother.

"That's fine," said Gaylen as he flew uncomfortably past the weeping and consoling women on the floor. "I'm really sorry Rebecca," he said, "you deserve better."

"Thank you. I will find you tomorrow," said Mother as Gaylen closed the door behind him.

"It was true," I cried after the front door closed. "Everything they were saying was true. No rich boy is going to fall in love with a poor girl. It's just a human tale. Princes don't fall for peasants in real life; at least not without a very strong pre-nuptial agreement. I can't believe I fell for it. I'm so stupid. I really thought he loved me."

"Honestly, Sweetie, I think he did," Mother said while she rocked me in her arms.

"Then where is he?" I asked.

"Most likely wherever his parents want him to be," she answered. Then she squeezed my shoulders tightly for a moment and released her hold. She caressed my face as she stood up and straightened her posture. "I think it's time you knew who your father was."

CHAPTER TWENTY-FOUR

Mother's Little Secret

Mother rose from the floor and glided toward the stairs as I tipped my watery face in her direction. She had a unique ability to stop me from crying but this last statement worked better than anything before. The feeling of finally knowing who my father was, or is, immediately shut out any pain I had. I probably could have had a limb amputated and not felt it. I slid from my knees and sat on the floor as Mother came back down the stairs with an old cigar box that contained a small file folder. She sat before me, placed the box on the floor, removed a photo of a family and handed it to me.

"I was raised in New Orleans, Louisiana," she began. "My family didn't have much money. I had a brother and a sister; Henry and Suzanne. I was the oldest, then Henry, Suzanne was the youngest. Momma was very good with a needle and thread and made most of our clothes. Suzanne and I always had three dresses each and Henry had three shirts and two pair of pants.

"When we were young, Suzanne and I would sneak off with Henry's pants when we wanted to play games with the boys. It wasn't proper to wear a dress back then if you were going to be flying around with boys. I wasn't very fast but still enjoyed picking on the boys. Neither Momma nor Henry was pleased when we borrowed the pants and, looking back, I realize that it wasn't fair to him since he had no desire to wear our dresses. When Suzanne and I got older, we couldn't really wear Henry's clothes anymore but she and I were about the same size so we would share our dresses with each other. Having six dresses to rotate made us seem less poor.

"Both Momma and Daddy knew the value of an education. I made the most of the public school system and got straight A's all through high school. I was valedictorian of our class and received a scholarship to secondary school in Augusta, Georgia. Georgia was a long way from Louisiana; a long, long way, but it was the best school for what I wanted to study. I was going to be a botanist and had earned a scholarship so I went. I loved school. I loved learning new things and meeting new fairies. I was doing very well. I designed a plant that was only three feet tall but would process more carbon dioxide than a pine tree. Five plants would create the oxygen needed for one human to survive for a year. I had offers from three different colonies to come and redevelop their farms. But then I met your father.

"His name was Quay. He was smart and witty and handsome. He had long, brown hair—I never liked green or red hair on men—broad shoulders, a nice, tight butt, and strong but gentle hands. He could do anything. He could color leaves more beautifully than any fairy I have ever seen. And, of course, he was on the flying team. I'm sure that's where you got most of your athleticism because my family didn't do much more than fish and drink nectar. So, anyway, how could I not fall in love?" She paused when she saw the look of disbelief on my face.

"Yes, I have been in love," she added. "I know the feeling of being with someone who makes you feel special and comfortable and safe. I know how it feels when their hand grasps yours and you close your own hand around theirs creating that simple but noticeable bond. I remember feeling energized when he took a quick moment in passing to give me a kiss on the cheek to show his affection. I remember dancing and feeling so peaceful that I had to lock my fingers behind his neck so my limp arms didn't just flop down in front of me. I remember not being able to keep my eyes open and the only thing keeping my head from dropping onto his chest was his forehead leaning against mine. Love is being at true and total peace with the one you are with. It is hoping that this peace, this person, will always be there for you and that you, as you are, create the same peace in them. I have been in love, Rebecca. I just couldn't afford to be in love these last eighteen years."

I watched her facial expressions go from bliss to sadness while she allowed herself to remember those feelings she had repressed for so many years. Her eem was stronger than I had ever experienced from anyone. I had to remind myself to breathe as I sat helplessly waiting for the next sentence. Mother gathered her emotions, cleared her throat and continued.

"We wanted to get married but he came from a very wealthy family in the Atlanta area and there was no way they were going to let him marry a poor girl from Louisiana who only owned five dresses that she made herself…'What would the women at the club say?'… I still remember our last date. We spent the entire night flying through the trees and looking at the stars and holding each other. There was a kiss and more kisses and we woke up in each other's arms in a cluster of azalea bushes.

"Later that day, after a long argument with his mother and father who threatened to disown him, Quay told me he couldn't see me anymore. Two weeks later I went to his home to tell him I was pregnant. He wasn't there so I left him a letter saying I didn't want anything from him and that I just thought he should know. The truth was I still loved him and I would have much preferred raising his child with him.

"For the next four months, I dealt only with their family representative who made sure my medical bills were paid and presented me with twenty gold stones in exchange for my signature on a contract stating I would never reveal the name of your father.

"I saw your father one last time. It was the day before you were born. Had he seen you, I doubt he would have been able to leave. He came to me in the hospital and gave me another ten gold stones. It was all he had. His family had no idea he had done it. That money was to take care of us for as long as it would last. And, at that very moment, I vowed that you would not be treated like me. You would not be considered poor or low class. You would speak more eloquently than those educated in the private schools. You would walk more gracefully than any human and you would have the feminine skills to capture any man that you wanted. But most importantly, you would not be poor.

"I knew that we couldn't stay in Georgia. We needed a fresh start and you needed to be in a place where nobody knew that your father had abandoned us. I stuffed you and three dresses into a frontpack and flew west toward Louisiana. You were a wonderful passenger. You barely made a sound through Alabama and Mississippi and seemed to like it best when we were flying fast. As we crossed over the great river, I searched for the sense of comfort I remembered from my youth. But it never came.

"It may have still been there but I had changed too much to feel it. I only knew that this place no longer felt like home. I stopped in a willow tree to rest and feed you. I looked down at your beautiful face and imagined you growing up in this humid climate with bugs and wild cats and poisonous snakes and wondered what you would say about all of it if you could speak. And almost as if you were reading my mind, your face became serious, you looked directly into my eyes and our eems connected for the first time. You wanted to keep flying.

"We continued west and north stopping to rest and eat and open ourselves up to experience the places we passed through; wondering which place would grab us emotionally in a way that made us not want to leave. "Nothing captured our attention until we saw the mountains. It was as if they called to us. There before us stood this silhouette that never seemed to get nearer regardless of how long or fast I flew. And when we finally reached them, they became a wall that denied us the right to run from our past any longer. After experiencing a trip that anyone but a Traveler Fairy would admire, we were home. We were accepted into this colony and I cautiously began building your portfolio.

"In that box is a list of your bank accounts and

investments I made on your behalf. You own the tree this house is in and another acre of woods which includes the school's Touch-and-Go field. They rent it from you. I had hoped to have water rights from the creek to round out the portfolio but haven't had much luck. Altogether, you may be the wealthiest fairy in the colony. You have secretly helped about ten percent of this colony's businesses get started including each of the men who built my bedroom."

I flashed back to the night she threw me out into a windy, snowy night and what I said to deserve the banishment. "I'm so sorry," I said. She obviously did deserve better. One question grew stronger and stronger as I thumbed through the financial documents.

"I minored in finance," Mother said before I could ask. "I always thought I would start my own business some day." She stood and watched as I shuffled papers around with no clue of what I was looking at. "Would you like me to explain all of this?"

"Will it take long?" I asked.

"I imagine most of the night."

"Okay," I signed as I rose from the floor and brushed off my gown. "I don't expect I need to be quite so formal, do I?"

"I'm so sorry, Honey," she said. "Things will get better."

I fluttered to Mother, wrapped my arms around her and said, "They already have." I gave her a hug and added, "I love you."

She hugged me back and said, "I love you, too."

Suddenly there was a loud knock on the front door and a familiar voice hollered, "Rebecca, what'cha doin'?"

Older and Wiser

*B*rent and I started tooth fairy training the next week. We saw each other very little during the night but always made time to fly home together after our shift and, on occasion, have breakfast near the stream. After a couple weeks he goaded me into a game of Touch-and-Go for old time's sake. We lined up at the same spot where we used to start as kids. I looked at the intense face of the man who had always been there for me and I smiled. I didn't want to race him. All I could see was a partnership. I remembered the times of playing together as a team and wanted that feeling of comaraderie but on a higher level. He called "touch" as he poked me on the head and darted toward the safe spot. I just fluttered in place. I had finally realized that my true safe spot was wherever he was.

After a moment Brent realized I wasn't beside him. He stopped and turned to see me in the same place we started and rushed back to check on me.

"Are you alright?" he asked. He was always concerned about my wellbeing.

"I'm fine," I said. "Go ahead and win. I'll be right here."

"You want to be caught?" Brent asked, confused. "You want me to catch you?" he confirmed.

"I think it's about time, don't you?" I said impishly.

It took a few minutes for Brent to consider what was happening. Though each of us was attracted to the other at some time in our lives, neither of us was willing to make it known until now. I stared calmly into his eyes and he into mine as our eems connected and we shared the many levels of love and friendship we had for each other; the love and friendship that had kept us emotionally close over many years and now pulled us physically close for the first time.

"Yes, I do," he said coolly. I wasn't surprised that he was also a good kisser.

We had a new house built in a Maple tree on the edge of the school's Touch-and-Go field and gave Mother the house I grew up in and twenty-five percent of the money she saved for me—she refused to take half. She used the money to buy some nice things for the house and some new clothes. She now allows herself to have up to ten dresses at a time. My wealth no longer a secret, Brent and I found ourselves attending charity functions and seasonal balls where I walked as gracefully as a human. Lake's family fell on hard times and had to sell their water rights to the creek. Because the economy was tough for everyone, Mother was able to get them for a very good price. All of it eventually became mine when Mother passed on two years ago.

Mother and I were very close. I even called her "Mom" on occasion without repercussion. I miss her. I miss her strong eem and the bond we shared. I didn't realize how close we had become until she died and I found myself wanting to talk with her about the great loss I was experiencing.

I once heard a wise fairy say "When I was fifteen, I couldn't believe how stupid my parents were. When I turned twenty-five, I couldn't believe how much they had learned in ten years." Now that I am older, I understand what that statement really means.

Some of the most difficult phases of our lives come when we are also trying to establish our independence from our parents. We pull away from the people who want to help us the most and seek advice from those closer to our own age who also happen to be going through the same trials and who are equally ignorant. We truly become the blind leading the blind. Life will never be easy but it also doesn't have to be as hard as we tend to make it.

I hope that I made the most of those times when my eem was strongest with fairies other than my mom.

Sharing your life experiences with others is still the most important thing about living. The best way to share is through our eems. Only after you have flown with another's wings can you truly understand them. That's what eeming is. I have worked very hard to improve my eeming skills and have made it my life's goal to be able to look everyone—fairy or human—in the eye and say, with honesty and compassion, "I'm eeming you."

BIOGRAPHY

**Paul Vincent Rodriguez** was raised in the small town of Alma, Michigan. He spent a lot of time in the woods of the northern Lower Peninsula where nature had not yet been disturbed and where magical creatures prevail. It wasn't until he had children that he found that magic is everywhere—even in cities. It is his hope that someday, everyone will be able to see the magic too.

Coming Soon

TALES OF FAIRIES

The Tale of
Darvin
THE Nerd

TALES OF FAIRIES

The Tale of
Flaylen
THE Fallen

www.ingramcontent.com/pod-product-compliance
Lightning Source LLC
Chambersburg PA
CBHW021104130626
46554CB00002B/530